STEALING FROM MR. RICH

BILLIONAIRE HEISTS #1

ANNA HACKETT

Stealing from Mr. Rich

Published by Anna Hackett

Copyright 2021 by Anna Hackett

Cover by RBA Designs

Cover image by Wander Aguiar

Edits by Tanya Saari

ISBN (ebook): 978-1-922414-29-8

ISBN (paperback): 978-1-922414-30-4

This book is a work of fiction. All names, characters, places and incidents are either the product of the author's imagination or are used fictitiously. Any resemblance to actual persons, events or places is coincidental. No part of this book may be reproduced, scanned, or distributed in any printed or electronic form.

WHAT READERS ARE SAYING ABOUT ANNA'S ACTION ROMANCE

Heart of Eon - Romantic Book of the Year (Ruby) winner 2020

Cyborg - PRISM Award Winner 2019

Edge of Eon and Mission: Her Protection - Romantic Book of the Year (Ruby) finalists 2019

Unfathomed and Unmapped - Romantic Book of the Year (Ruby) finalists 2018

Unexplored – Romantic Book of the Year (Ruby) Novella Winner 2017

Return to Dark Earth – One of Library Journal's Best E-Original Books for 2015 and two-time SFR Galaxy Awards winner

At Star's End – One of Library Journal's Best E-Original Romances for 2014

The Phoenix Adventures – SFR Galaxy Award Winner for Most Fun New Series and "Why Isn't This a Movie?" Series

Beneath a Trojan Moon – SFR Galaxy Award Winner and RWAus Ella Award Winner

Hell Squad – SFR Galaxy Award for best Post-Apocalypse for Readers who don't like Post-Apocalypse

"Like Indiana Jones meets Star Wars. A treasure hunt with a steamy romance." – SFF Dragon, review of *Among Galactic Ruins*

"Action, danger, aliens, romance – yup, it's another great book from Anna Hackett!" – Book Gannet Reviews, review of *Hell Squad: Marcus*

Sign up for my VIP mailing list and get your *free box set* containing three action-packed romances.

Visit here to get started: www.annahackett.com

1

BROTHER IN TROUBLE

Monroe

The old-fashioned Rosengrens safe was a beauty.

I carefully turned the combination dial, then pressed closer to the safe. The metal was cool under my fingertips. The safe wasn't pretty, but stout and secure. There was something to be said for solid security.

Rosengrens had started making safes in Sweden over a hundred years ago. They were good at it. I listened to the pins, waiting for contact. Newer safes had internals made from lightweight materials to reduce sensory feedback, so I didn't get to use these skills very often.

Some people could play the piano, I could play a safe. The tiny vibration I was waiting for reached my fingertips, followed by the faintest click.

"I've gotcha, old girl." The Rosengrens had quite a few quirks, but my blood sang as I moved the dial again.

I heard a louder click and spun the handle.

1

The safe door swung open. Inside, I saw stacks of jewelry cases and wads of hundred-dollar bills. *Nice.*

Standing, I dusted my hands off on my jeans. "There you go, Mr. Goldstein."

"You are a doll, Monroe O'Connor. Thank you."

The older man, dressed neatly in pressed chinos and a blue shirt, grinned at me. He had coke-bottle glasses, wispy, white hair, and a wrinkled face.

I smiled at him. Mr. Goldstein was one of my favorite people. "I'll send you my bill."

His grin widened. "I don't know what I'd do without you."

I raised a brow. "You could stop forgetting your safe combination."

The wealthy old man called me every month or so to open his safe. Right now, we were standing in the home office of his expensive Park Avenue penthouse.

It was decorated in what I thought of as "rich, old man." There were heavy drapes, gold-framed artwork, lots of dark wood—including the built-in shelves around the safe—and a huge desk.

"Then I wouldn't get to see your pretty face," he said.

I smiled and patted his shoulder. "I'll see you next month, Mr. Goldstein." The poor man was lonely. His wife had died the year before, and his only son lived in Europe.

"Sure thing, Monroe. I'll have some of those donuts you like."

We headed for the front door and my chest tightened. I understood feeling lonely. "You could do with some new locks on your door. I mean, your building has top-notch security, but you can never be too careful. Pop by the shop if you want to talk locks."

He beamed at me and held the door open. "I might do that."

"Bye, Mr. Goldstein."

I headed down the plush hall to the elevator. Everything in the building screamed old money. I felt like an imposter just being in the building. Like I had "daughter of a criminal" stamped on my head.

Pulling out my cell phone, I pulled up my accounting app and entered Mr. Goldstein's callout. Next, I checked my messages.

Still nothing from Maguire.

Frowning, I bit my lip. That made it three days since I'd heard from my little brother. I shot him off a quick text.

"Text me back, Mag," I muttered.

The elevator opened and I stepped in, trying not to worry about Maguire. He was an adult, but I'd practically raised him. Most days it felt like I had a twenty-four-year-old kid.

The elevator slowed and stopped at another floor. An older, well-dressed couple entered. They eyed me and my well-worn jeans like I'd crawled out from under a rock.

I smiled. "Good morning."

Yeah, yeah, I'm not wearing designer duds, and my bank account doesn't have a gazillion zeros. You're so much better than me.

Ignoring them, I scrolled through Instagram. When we finally reached the lobby, the couple shot me another dubious look before they left. I strode out across the marble-lined space and rolled my eyes.

During my teens, I'd cared about what people thought. Everyone had known that my father was Terry O'Connor—expert thief, safecracker, and con man. I'd felt every repulsed look and sly smirk at high school.

Then I'd grown up, cultivated some thicker skin, and learned not to care. *Fuck 'em.* People who looked down on others for things outside their control were assholes.

I wrinkled my nose. Okay, it was easier said than done.

When I walked outside, the street was busy. I smiled, breathing in the scent of New York—car exhaust, burnt meat, and rotting trash. Besides, most people cared more about themselves. They judged you, left you bleeding, then forgot you in the blink of an eye.

I unlocked my bicycle, and pulled on my helmet, then set off down the street. I needed to get to the store. The ride wasn't long, but I spent every second worrying about Mag.

My brother had a knack for finding trouble. I sighed. After a childhood, where both our mothers had taken off, and Da was in and out of jail, Mag was entitled to being a bit messed up. The O'Connors were a long way from the Brady Bunch.

I pulled up in front of my shop in Hell's Kitchen and stopped for a second.

I grinned. *All mine.*

Okay, I didn't own the building, but I owned the store. The sign above the shop said *Lady Locksmith*. The logo was lipstick red—a woman's hand with gorgeous red nails, holding a set of keys.

After I locked up my bike, I strode inside. A chime sounded.

God, I loved the place. It was filled with glossy, warm-wood shelves lined with displays of state-of-the-art locks and safes. A key-cutting machine sat at the back.

A blonde head popped up from behind a long, shiny counter.

"You're back," Sabrina said.

My best friend looked like a doll—small, petite, with a head of golden curls.

We'd met doing our business degrees at college, and had become fast friends. Sabrina had always wanted to be tall and sexy, but had to settle for small and cute. She was my manager, and was getting married in a month.

"Yeah, Mr. Goldstein forgot his safe code again," I said.

Sabrina snorted. "That old coot doesn't forget, he just likes looking at your ass."

"He's harmless. He's nice, and lonely. How's the team doing?"

Sabrina leaned forward, pulling out her tablet. I often wondered if she slept with it. "Liz is out back unpacking stock." Sabrina's nose wrinkled. "McRoberts overcharged us on the Schlage locks again."

"That prick." He was always trying to screw me over. "I'll call him."

"Paola, Kat, and Isabella are all out on jobs."

Excellent. Business was doing well. Lady Locksmith specialized in providing female locksmiths to all the single ladies of New York. They also advised on how to keep them safe—securing locks, doors, and windows.

I had a dream of one day seeing multiple Lady Locksmiths around the city. Hell, around every city. A girl could dream. Growing up, once I understood the damage my father did to other people, all I'd wanted was to be respectable. To earn my own way and add to the world, not take from it.

"Did you get that new article I sent you to post on the blog?" I asked.

Sabrina nodded. "It'll go live shortly, and then I'll post on Insta, as well."

When I had the time, I wrote articles on how women —single *and* married—should secure their homes. My latest was aimed at domestic-violence survivors, and helping them feel safe. I donated my time to Nightingale House, a local shelter that helped women leaving DV situations, and I installed locks for them, free of charge.

"We should start a podcast," Sabrina said.

I wrinkled my nose. "I don't have time to sit around recording stuff." I did my fair share of callouts for jobs, plus at night I had to stay on top of the business-side of the store.

"Fine, fine." Sabrina leaned against the counter and eyed my jeans. "Damn, I hate you for being tall, long, and gorgeous. You're going to look *way* too beautiful as my maid of honor." She waved a hand between us. "You're all tall, sleek, and dark-haired, and I'm...the opposite."

I had some distant Black Irish ancestor to thank for my pale skin and ink-black hair. Growing up, I wanted to be short, blonde, and tanned. I snorted. "Beauty comes in all different forms, Sabrina." I gripped her shoulders. "You are so damn pretty, and your fiancé happens to think you are the most beautiful woman in the world. Andrew is gaga over you."

Sabrina sighed happily. "He does and he is." A pause. "So, do you have a date for my wedding yet?" My bestie's voice turned breezy and casual.

Uh-oh. I froze. All the wedding prep had sent my normally easygoing best friend a bit crazy. And I knew very well not to trust that tone.

I edged toward my office. "Not yet."

Sabrina's blue eyes sparked. "It's only *four* weeks away, Monroe. The maid of honor can't come alone."

"I'll be busy helping you out—"

"Find a date, Monroe."

"I don't want to just pick anyone for your wedding—"

Sabrina stomped her foot. "Find someone, or I'll find someone for you."

I held up my hands. "Okay, okay." I headed for my office. "I'll—" My cell phone rang. *Yes.* "I've got a call. Got to go." I dove through the office door.

"I won't forget," Sabrina yelled. "I'll revoke your best-friend status, if I have to."

I closed the door on my bridezilla bestie and looked at the phone.

Maguire. Finally.

I stabbed the call button. "Where have you been?"

"We have your brother," a robotic voice said.

My blood ran cold. My chest felt like it had filled with concrete.

"If you want to keep him alive, you'll do exactly as I say."

Zane

God, this party was boring.

Zane Roth sipped his wine and glanced around the ballroom at the Mandarin Oriental. The party held the Who's Who of New York society, all dressed up in their glittering best. The ceiling shimmered with a sea of crystal lights, tall flower arrangements dominated the tables, and the wall of windows had a great view of the Manhattan skyline.

Everything was picture perfect...and boring.

If it wasn't for the charity auction, he wouldn't be dressed in his tuxedo and dodging annoying people.

"I'm so sick of these parties," he muttered.

A snort came from beside him.

One of his best friends, Maverick Rivera, sipped his wine. "You were voted New York's sexiest billionaire bachelor. You should be loving this shindig."

Mav had been one of his best friends since college. Like Zane, Maverick hadn't come from wealth. They'd both earned it the old-fashioned way. Zane loved numbers and money, and had made Wall Street his hunting ground. Mav was a geek, despite not looking like a stereotypical one. He'd grown up in a strong, Mexican-American family, and with his brown skin, broad shoulders, and the fact that he worked out a lot, no one would pick him for a tech billionaire.

But under the big body, the man was a computer geek to the bone.

"All the society mamas are giving you lots of speculative looks." Mav gave him a small grin.

"Shut it, Rivera."

"They're all dreaming of marrying their daughters off to billionaire Zane Roth, the finance King of Wall Street."

Zane glared. "You done?"

"Oh, I could go on."

"I seem to recall another article about the billionaire bachelors. All three of us." Zane tipped his glass at his friend. "They'll be coming for you, next."

Mav's smile dissolved, and he shrugged a broad shoulder. "I'll toss Kensington at them. He's pretty."

Liam Kensington was the third member of their trio. Unlike Zane and Mav, Liam had come from money, although he worked hard to avoid his bloodsucking family.

Zane saw a woman in a slinky, blue dress shoot him a welcoming smile.

He looked away.

When he'd made his first billion, he'd welcomed the attention. Especially the female attention. He'd bedded more than his fair share of gorgeous women.

Of late, nothing and no one caught his interest. Women all left him feeling numb.

Work. He thrived on that.

A part of him figured he'd never find a woman who made him feel the same way as his work.

"Speak of the devil," Mav said.

Zane looked up to see Liam Kensington striding toward them. With the lean body of a swimmer, clad in a perfectly tailored tuxedo, he looked every inch the billionaire. His gold hair complemented a face the ladies oohed over.

People tried to get his attention, but the real estate mogul ignored everyone.

He reached Zane and Mav, grabbed Zane's wine, and emptied it in two gulps.

"I hate this party. When can we leave?" Having spent his formative years in London, he had a posh British accent. Another thing the ladies loved. "I have a contract to work on, my fundraiser ball to plan, and things to catch up on after our trip to San Francisco."

The three of them had just returned from a business trip to the West Coast.

"Can't leave until the auction's done," Zane said.

Liam sighed. His handsome face often had him voted the best-looking billionaire bachelor.

"Buy up big," Zane said. "Proceeds go to the Boys and Girls Clubs."

"One of your pet charities," Liam said.

"Yeah." Zane's father had left when he was seven. His mom had worked hard to support them. She was his hero. He liked to give back to charities that supported kids growing up in tough circumstances.

He'd set his mom up in a gorgeous house Upstate that she loved. And he was here for her tonight.

"Don't bid on the Phillips-Morley necklace, though," he added. "It's mine."

The necklace had a huge, rectangular sapphire pendant surrounded by diamonds. It was the real-life necklace said to have inspired the necklace in the movie, *Titanic*. It had been given to a young woman, Kate Florence Phillips, by her lover, Henry Samuel Morley. The two had run away together and booked passage on the Titanic.

Unfortunately for poor Kate, Henry had drowned when the ship had sunk. She'd returned to England with the necklace and a baby in her belly.

Zane's mother had always loved the story and pored over pictures of the necklace. She'd told him the story of the lovers, over and over.

"It was a gift from a man to a woman he loved. She was a shop girl, and he owned the store, but they fell in love, even though society frowned on their love." She sighed. "That's true love, Zane. Devotion, loyalty, through the good times and the bad."

Everything Carol Roth had never known.

Of course, it turned out old Henry was much older than his lover, and already married. But Zane didn't want to ruin the fairy tale for his mom.

Now, the Phillips-Morley necklace had turned up, and was being offered at auction. And Zane was going to get it for his mom. It was her birthday in a few months.

"Hey, is your fancy, new safe ready yet?" Zane asked Mav.

His friend nodded. "You're getting one of the first ones. I can have my team install it this week."

"Perfect." Mav's new Riv3000 was the latest in high-tech safes and said to be unbreakable. "I'll keep the necklace in it until my mom's birthday."

Someone called out Liam's name. With a sigh, their friend forced a smile. "Can't dodge this one. Simpson's an investor in my Brooklyn project. I'll be back."

"Need a refill?" Zane asked Mav.

"Sure."

Zane headed for the bar. He'd almost reached it when a manicured hand snagged his arm.

"Zane."

He looked down at the woman and barely swallowed his groan. "Allegra. You look lovely this evening."

She did. Allegra Montgomery's shimmery, silver dress hugged her slender figure, and her cloud of mahogany brown hair accented her beautiful face. As the only daughter of a wealthy New York family—her father was from *the* Montgomery family and her mother was a former Miss America—Allegra was well-bred and well-educated but also, as he'd discovered, spoiled and liked getting her way.

Her dark eyes bored into him. "I'm sorry things ended badly for us the other month. I was..." Her voice lowered, and she stroked his forearm. "I miss you. I was hoping we could catch up again."

Zane arched a brow. They'd dated for a few weeks, shared a few dinners, and some decent sex. But Allegra liked being the center of attention, complained that he worked too much, and had constantly hounded him to take her on vacation. Preferably on a private jet to Tahiti or the Maldives.

When she'd asked him if it would be too much for him to give her a credit card of her own, for monthly expenses, Zane had exited stage left.

"I don't think so, Allegra. We aren't...compatible."

Her full lips turned into a pout. "I thought we were *very* compatible."

He cleared his throat. "I heard you moved on. With Chip Huffington."

Allegra waved a hand. "Oh, that's nothing serious."

And Chip was only a millionaire. Allegra would see that as a step down. In fact, Zane felt like every time she looked at him, he could almost see little dollar signs in her eyes.

He dredged up a smile. "I wish you all the best, Allegra. Good evening." He sidestepped her and made a beeline for the bar.

"What can I get you?" the bartender asked.

Wine wasn't going to cut it. It would probably be frowned on to ask for an entire bottle of Scotch. "Two glasses of Scotch, please. On the rocks. Do you have Macallan?"

"No, sorry, sir. Will Glenfiddich do?"

"Sure."

"Ladies and gentlemen," a voice said over the loudspeaker. The lights lowered. "I hope you're ready to spend big for a wonderful cause."

Carrying the drinks, Zane hurried back to Mav and Liam. He handed Mav a glass.

"Let's do this," Mav grumbled. "And next time, I'll make a generous online donation so I don't have to come to the party."

"Drinks at my place after I get the necklace," Zane said. "I have a very good bottle of Macallan."

Mav stilled. "How good?"

"Macallan 25. Single malt."

"I'm there," Liam said.

Mav lifted his chin.

Ahead, Zane watched the evening's host lift a black cloth off a pedestal. He stared at the necklace, the sapphire glittering under the lights.

There it was.

The sapphire was a deep, rich blue. Just like all the photos his mother had shown him.

"Get that damn necklace, Roth, and let's get out of here," Mav said.

Zane nodded. He'd get the necklace for the one woman in his life who rarely asked for anything, then escape the rest of the bloodsuckers and hang with his friends.

2

I'LL WRITE YOU A CHECK

Monroe

"Lady, you sure you want to get out here?" the cabbie drawled.

My belly turned circles, then curled up in the fetal position. *Hell, no.*

We were down by the warehouses by the water in Red Hook, Brooklyn. Night was settling over the city and this was *not* a good place to be. There were no people around, or at least, not nice ones, and there were lots of shadows. Really dark ones.

I shoved money at the man.

"No, but I don't have a choice." I climbed out and then gripped the strap of my backpack.

What the hell have you got yourself mixed up in now, Mag?

Fear and anger for my brother warred in my chest.

I was going to find him, get him safe, then smack him around the ears.

I walked along the row of creepy warehouses, looking for Warehouse Seven.

That's what they'd told me. The eerie, robot voice. My boots echoed on the dirty concrete. I smelled the water, and the scent of something rotting.

Mouth dry, I approached the warehouse. A man stepped out of the shadows. He was big, bulky, and wore a dark suit. He had that blank look that said he'd punch you in the face and not feel bad about it.

He eyed me for a second, then opened the metal door in the side of the warehouse and jerked his head.

A man of no words.

Curbing my nerves, I stepped inside the warehouse. It was dark and appropriately creepy. I lifted my chin and refused to show the fear crawling through my insides.

Ahead, a single bright light sat on a card table, back-lighting the silhouettes of several men in suits.

As I approached, they shifted, and I saw a slimmer figure tied to a chair.

Mag. He was illuminated by a bright light.

"Maguire." My stomach plummeted.

My brother's wild, panicked eyes met mine. He had a gag tied around his mouth. He looked tired and stressed, his normally thick, dark hair lank.

Oh, God. The taste of bile surged into my mouth.

I took two steps toward him, but a goon's arm shot out and stopped me.

My hands balled into fists. I sensed more people shifting in the shadows around me. I made myself take a few deep breaths. *Keep it together, Monroe.*

There was a man in the shadows right behind Maguire.

"Ms. O'Connor, I'm glad you came."

The voice had an accent. Russian. *Damn you, Mag.* Whatever this was, it was really, really bad.

I lifted my chin and swallowed. "I just want my brother."

"It's not that simple."

"You untie him. We go. He won't bother you again. That's simple enough."

I saw a flash of white teeth in the darkness. "He owes me money."

My nails bit into my palms. I reached for my backpack. "I'll write you a check."

I had some savings, for my business, but I had to get Maguire out of this mess.

The shadowed man laughed, and I froze. A shiver had goosebumps breaking out on the back of my neck.

Mag made a choked sound around his gag.

"Your brother's been trying his hand at gambling, Ms. O'Connor. He owes me a hundred thousand dollars."

"What?" I felt like the floor heaved under my feet. I couldn't process it. *A hundred thousand dollars?*

Mag barely held down a part-time job. He usually picked up odd jobs here and there. He didn't have that kind of money. I didn't have that kind of money.

My brother made another sound, and looked at the concrete floor, not meeting my gaze.

"Can you write me a check for that?" Mr. Shadow asked.

My throat was so tight it felt like I was being strangled. *Damn you, Maguire.* I stared at the top of his bent head. I was going to kill him myself...if we got out of this alive.

I squeezed my eyes closed. "No." My voice was a scratchy whisper.

"Until I get what I want, your brother's life is mine."

I opened my eyes. "What do you want?" I asked woodenly.

"I want you to get something for me."

My stomach dropped. I should have known.

I felt a familiar weight slam down on me. No matter how hard I tried to escape the past, it always dragged me back.

The muck was deep in my skin, and it would never wash off.

I could get a college degree, own my own business, work my butt off, but I could never get free of my family's murky legacy.

Resignation made me feel so damn tired. "You want me to steal something."

"Your brother has told us that you've inherited your father's unique skills. In finessing safes. In fact, he thinks you're better than your father."

I glanced at Mag. He was looking at me now with pleading gray eyes the same color as my own—full of misery and sorrow.

I looked away, staring at the scarred walls—I felt too raw to comfort him right now.

"I get this thing for you, you set my brother free and unharmed. Then you'll *never* contact him again."

"Yes." Then shadow man shrugged. "Although, if he comes looking for a game..."

"You'll *never* see him again." I dragged air into my burning lungs. "What do you want me to steal?"

God, I felt like I was going to be sick. I'd vowed, for years, to never, ever turn into my father.

"The Phillips-Morley necklace."

My chest tightened. I hadn't heard of it, but no doubt it was priceless. "I'm guessing that's worth more than a hundred thousand dollars."

"That's the deal." There was iron in the man's voice.

I rubbed my temple. "Where is it?"

"Being purchased tonight at a charity auction by Zane Roth."

Oh. *Shit.* One of New York's billionaire bachelors.

"He'll be storing it in his new safe. A Rivera 3000."

Now I really was going to be sick. "No one can break into a Riv3000."

The man touched Mag's neck and my brother jerked. "Your brother's life depends on it, so you better make sure you can, Ms. O'Connor. You have one week."

Yep, I was going to kill my brother.

Zane

The hit slammed into his gut, driving the air out of him.

With a grunt, Zane dodged, but his attacker followed. The front kick sent him staggering.

Fuck. Zane whirled and swung his arm, keeping his

palm flat. The side of his hand chopped into his attacker's neck.

The wiry man spat out a curse and stepped back on the mats. Then he straightened. "That was better, Roth."

Simeon was all lean muscle, had a face with a ragged scar down his cheek, and gray hair he kept buzzed short. The trainer never pulled a punch...or a hit or kick. He didn't care that he was training billionaires. He taught them Krav Maga, and claimed he'd been in the Israeli military. Zane had his suspicions. If anyone was a former Mossad spy, it was this crusty guy.

Zane rubbed his gut. "Did you have to kick me so hard?"

"You weren't paying attention." Simeon raised a brow. "You told me you didn't want a bodyguard following you around, so you need to pay attention to your surroundings. And practice your skills."

Zane had security on call, but he hadn't wanted some bodyguard with him twenty-four-seven. Liam and Mav felt the same. They all paid a small fortune to secure their businesses and properties, and they also paid Simeon a lot of money to beat them up a few times a week, so they could all hold their own in a fight.

Simeon wiggled his fingers. "Again."

With a growl, Zane attacked. They crossed the mats, kicking, blocking, hitting, and deflecting. Zane got behind Simeon and grabbed him in a chokehold. Now, if he could get the man down—

Bam.

Zane found himself flat on his back on the mats,

staring at the ceiling of the large gym. Simeon had tossed him over his shoulder.

Chuckles broke out nearby.

Turning his head, Zane took in Mav and Liam. Both men were in harnesses and halfway up the massive climbing wall.

"That's going to bruise," Liam called out.

Mav just laughed.

"Fuck you," Zane muttered. "He's tossed both of you on your asses plenty of times before."

Simeon held out a hand and Zane let the trainer haul him up. He crossed to the bench at the side of the mats, grabbed a towel, wiped his face, then slung it around his neck. Next, he grabbed a bottle of water. As he drank it, he watched Liam and Mav get to the top of the wall.

Liam moved like the wind—easy, light, like he was weightless. He dared some risky jumps to out-of-reach handholds, and looked like magic doing it. Mav was bigger and bulkier, and was an aggressive climber. He used his strength to power up the wall.

Zane blew out a breath, feeling a strange restlessness. He shrugged his shoulders to release the tension. Work was good, he had nothing to complain about.

He also had the necklace for his mom, and had helped out a great charity in the process.

"You okay?"

Zane looked up to see Simeon watching him.

"I'm fine."

"Heard you broke up with that latest woman you were seeing?"

Zane shrugged. "It wasn't serious, and it was no loss. She liked my money more than me."

Simeon grunted. Across the gym, Liam and Mav were back on the mats and unclipping their harnesses.

"You need a good woman," Simeon said.

Zane laughed. "What do you know about good women?" He imagined that Simeon lived in a dark cave, lifting weights and gnawing raw meat.

"I have one. Married for thirty-five years. Best thing that ever happened to me."

Zane blinked. "You're married?"

A smile lifted the corners of Simeon's lips. "Yes. When it's the right one, she makes everything better."

Liam and Mav joined them, but Zane kept his gaze on the older man. "I don't know, success seems to have made it harder to find good people."

"You don't find the right woman, Zane, it just happens."

That sounded awfully Zen and new age for his grizzled Krav Maga trainer. Beside them, Mav snorted.

"How did you know your wife was the right one?" Zane asked.

Simeon slammed a fist against his hard stomach. "You feel it here. I knew the first moment I set eyes on my Talia." Simeon's gaze turned inward, his smile widening. "We crashed our cars in a parking lot. She rear-ended me. Wasn't watching where she was going."

Liam grinned. "Is that how she tells it?"

Simeon laughed. "Hell, no. She claims to this day that it was all my fault." The trainer's gaze came back to Zane. "As she yelled at me, I knew. It took time to court her, to know all of her, but that first spark of knowing had already told me that she was mine."

Mav made a low sound. "And sometimes it's just lust, and it leads you down the wrong path."

"Kaitlyn was a conniving bitch, Mav," Zane said. "You've got to let it go."

"I have," Mav said. "Doesn't mean I'm going to run right back in there and take a stupid risk. I learn from my mistakes. That's what makes me good at my job." He shook his head. "I don't believe in love at first sight—"

"Not love at first sight," Simeon said. "*Knowing* at first sight. Love takes time. It needs to be tended and has to grow."

Mav grabbed his gym bag. "Nothing to grow if the seed's poisoned to start with." He huffed out a breath. "Roth, I need to take a scan of your fingerprint so my guys can code your new safe."

"Great." The quicker it was installed, the better. Zane was keeping the necklace in his safe at work for the moment.

Mav pulled out a tablet. It was wafer-thin and had the Rivera Tech logo—a stylized swirl of a river—on it. No doubt the tablet was some experimental prototype that Mav had cooked up and wasn't for sale. He could probably hack the Pentagon with it.

Zane pressed his finger to the screen and it flashed, then made a small beep.

"Done." Mav tucked the tablet away. "Can you put my guys on the list so your building security can let them in to do the installation?"

"Sure thing. Thanks, Mav."

Liam grabbed his bag. "I've got to get going. I've got a full day of meetings."

"Me too." Zane grabbed his gear, ready to hit the showers.

Simeon jerked his chin up. "Remember what I said, Zane."

"I don't forget anything you tell me, Sim. Especially when I've got the bruises and aches to remember you by."

The trainer barked out a laugh. "Get out of here."

Zane smiled and shook his head. He had no real interest in finding "the one." Lately, he was finding it tough to find a woman who captured his attention at all.

Time to get to work. Doing a successful deal gave him a sense of satisfaction, that would have to do for now.

Monroe

The morning dragged on as I finished unpacking locks at the back of Lady Locksmith. I was tired, because I'd slept like absolute crap. My nightmares had been filled with images of Mag—tied up, screaming, hurt.

I ran a hand over my face. One week. I had seven days to crack an unbreakable safe and steal from a billionaire. Shoving my tiredness and fear down deep, I tossed an empty cardboard box in the recycling bin.

It was still early. Sabrina wasn't coming in until later. I walked into my cramped, little office, and glanced at the newspaper on my desk. I felt like it was mocking me.

I picked it up.

The Phillips-Morley necklace was front and center. The thing was worth millions. Two of them to be exact.

I blew out a breath. There was also a picture of Zane Roth.

He was wearing a tuxedo, smiling, and looking as handsome as sin. My belly coiled. He had a strong jaw, and I was a sucker for a strong jaw. I'd always been a Superman fan.

I sighed. Superman would want nothing to do with the daughter of a criminal.

Hell, soon I'd be a criminal myself. Superman would cart me off to the police.

Despair tightened my throat. I'd fought so fucking hard to make a decent, law-abiding life for myself. To not be the criminal trash so many people assumed I'd be, like my father.

My mama says an apple never falls far from the tree.

You gonna grow up to be a criminal like your daddy, Monroe?

Watch your pockets, or the O'Connors are going to pick them.

The schoolyard taunts still stung, so many years later. Well, there was no time to feel sorry for myself. Mag was my brother, and no matter what, I loved him. I'd held his hand and taught him to cross the road. I'd walked him to school every day. I'd helped him with his homework, until he'd ended up helping me with mine because he was really good with numbers.

I had to save him.

Lifting the paper, I looked at Zane Roth's picture

again. He'd definitely want nothing to do with me. He moved in a completely different stratosphere.

There was another picture of him with his friends— the three billionaire bachelors of New York. All self-made. All attractive in their own ways. They worked hard, played hard, donated to their charities, and every single woman in the city would kill for an introduction.

I smoothed a hand over the picture of the necklace. Roth had bought it. Grabbing a notepad, I yanked it closer. I scribbled a few notes. I needed to know everything about it.

Sitting at my desk, I opened my aging laptop. *Diamond-encrusted sapphire.* I noted the weight and size. I couldn't leave anything to chance.

Then I found the story of Kate Florence Phillips. I found myself engrossed as I read about how old Henry Morley, twenty years older than her and married, had given the nineteen-year-old the necklace and convinced her to run away with him.

Poor, poor Kate. I shook my head. Men could not be trusted. They always took more than they gave.

Okay, enough on the necklace and gullible girls. Next, I tapped in a search and pulled up information on the Riv3000. It was a newly designed safe from Rivera Tech. Maverick Rivera was one of the billionaire bachelors and a bit of a guru with all things tech. I sold a line of Rivera Tech home safes and locks in my shop. They were good.

Shit. I bit my lip. They were touting the Riv3000 as burglar-proof and unbreakable.

Well, Da always said nothing was unbreakable.

The bell rang out in the store and I jumped up. I dredged up a smile for the middle-aged couple who'd entered. "Good morning."

They smiled at me. "We need some new locks, and you came highly recommended."

"Tell me what you're looking for." I helped the couple pick the right locks for their new apartment.

Back at my desk, I realized that I needed more information on the Riv3000, and on Zane Roth's penthouse.

I did a quick search and let out a whistle. Of course, the man lived on Billionaire's Row at the southern end of Central Park.

Roth owned a triplex penthouse in one of the new supertalls. In fact, 111 West 57th Street, also known as the Steinway Tower, was apparently the most-slender skyscraper in the world.

I saw there was a link to a spread on Roth's place in Forbes. I clicked it.

Damn. My heart stopped. It was *gorgeous.* The views of Central Park and the city were beyond breathtaking through a wall of glass. I clicked through the pictures, my stomach tight with envy. The master bedroom and bathroom were unreal. The third level was entirely what they called an open-air loggia, or what I'd call an amazing terrace.

I tried to imagine living in this place. I eyed the terrace and plunge pool, and sighed. I loved to swim. Some of the few good memories I had of my father was when he'd taken Mag and me to Coney Island to the beach.

Well, I sure didn't have a roof terrace pool. I didn't

even have a roof terrace, let alone a pool. I lived in the tiny apartment above Lady Locksmith. I didn't even have a bathtub.

The safe would be in his study. Tapping a finger against my lips, I studied the picture of the sleek office, with dark-gray walls and more brain-scrambling views. I considered all my options. No matter how great these photos were, I still needed to get inside and take a look around his place before the job.

And I had a good idea of how I was going to do that.

Okay. Now, the safe.

I grabbed my cell phone and dialed.

"What?" a male voice barked.

"Hi, Rollo."

A grunt. "Go away."

"Hey, I'm nice to you."

"You always want things."

"You enjoy the challenge. I need your help."

There was a long pause. "What?" Curiosity tinged his voice.

Rollo was a hacker who rarely left his basement apartment, was in love with his homemade computer, and loved hacking things.

"I need the schematics for a Riv3000 safe."

"What?" Rollo squawked. "You've lost it, sister."

"Come on, Rollo," I cajoled. "You can do anything, right?"

He sniffed.

"And I need a prototype of it."

"You're dreaming, O'Connor, or you've totally lost your mind."

"We both know your buddy, Bash, can whip something up if you give him the plans. In return, I'll bake you cupcakes. And those cookies you love, *and* a cheesecake."

Silence.

"That raspberry-and-white-chocolate cheesecake?" he asked.

"Yes."

A heavy sigh. "Okay, girly. I'll see what I can do."

I smiled. "I knew I could count on you."

"Extra chocolate chunks in those cookies."

"You got it, Rollo." I set the phone down and leaned back in my chair, chewing on my bottom lip.

Was Mag okay? My chest tightened. Were they feeding him, or was he hungry?

The shop door chimed again.

"Monroe," Sabrina called out. "I hope you're in there thinking about who to bring to my wedding?"

Sabrina sounded way too chirpy today. I pasted on a smile and walked through the office door. "Morning."

My best friend's brow creased. "You look like crap."

"Thanks. You look incredibly perky."

"Rough night?" Concern creased Sabrina's cute face. "Tell me that you were up all night having some hot sex."

I shot my friend a look.

Sabrina's shoulders sagged. "Or not."

"Mag's in a bind."

Sabrina let out a gusty sigh. "You need to stop bailing him out, Monroe, or he'll *never* grow up."

This was an old argument. "Sabrina—"

"Okay, okay." She held up a hand. "I won't say all the same things I've said a hundred times before. I know you love him, and Mag is lovable, but he needs to grow up."

"I need to head out for a bit." And plan how to break into a billionaire's multi-million-dollar penthouse, and crack his unbreakable, high-tech safe, and steal a priceless necklace.

I decided not to share those last bits with Sabrina.

"Sure." Sabrina grabbed some pamphlets on the counter and straightened them. "Grab me a mocha on the way back?"

"You got it," I replied.

Sabrina closed the distance, then wrapped her arms around me. The hug made tears prick in my eyes. There was no way in hell I'd drag my friend into the mess, but for a second, I didn't feel so alone. I held on tight, breathing in my friend's perfume.

Sabrina even smelled sunny and happy.

"Hey?" She leaned back, frowning. "You sure you're okay?"

"Peachy." I headed out the door before I lost it. "See you later."

3

UGLY, GRAY PANTS

Zane

Zane strode through the Roth Enterprises offices, and tried not to be amused as several new interns scurried to get out of his way.

The offices were all delineated with glass walls, and etched with the Roth Enterprises logo. The floors were sleek, cream marble, and the space was modern, with clean lines.

He nodded at Justin, his assistant, and stepped into his office.

It was big, with floor-to-ceiling windows showcasing a killer view of Lower Manhattan and the Woolworth Building.

He'd come a hell of a long way from the young man who'd made it through college on a bunch of scholarships and two part-time jobs.

This morning, he'd already sat through several meetings, had a long breakfast meeting with investors for a new development project, and fielded numerous phone calls.

The phone on his desk rang and he touched the speaker button. "Yes, Justin?"

"Mr. Roth, I have an assistant for a Prince Franz of Saxe-Bavaria on the line. The prince would like a business meeting with you. Apparently, he's looking for investors."

"No." It was common for anyone and everyone to come looking for Zane to be an investor, aka they wanted his money.

"And your mother is also on the line," Justin added.

"Put her through." Zane sat. "Hey, Mom."

"How's my boy?" His mother's warm voice came through the speaker.

It had just been the two of them for as long as he could remember. He realized that no matter how old he got, or what he achieved, he'd always be her little boy.

"I'm good. Busy. Look, Mom, I want you to come and stay with me for your birthday next month. I'll take you out for dinner." And give her the Phillips-Morley necklace.

"Are you going to bring a girl?"

Ah. His mom was always hopeful that he'd fall in love and make her a gaggle of grandchildren.

"No, Mom. Just you and me. We can have some special time together. You're my favorite girl."

His mother sighed. "Zane, just because your father didn't love us, doesn't mean all relationships are bad."

Zane pressed a hand to the back of his neck and grabbed the phone handset. "Mom, I date."

She made a scoffing sound. "Dinner and sex is not dating."

He winced. "I'm not discussing this with you."

"Fine." She didn't sound happy.

"Come down for your birthday. I'll book us a table at Le Bernadin." The restaurant was her favorite.

A small sigh. "All right, Zane. I love you."

"I love you too, Mom."

He'd just set the phone down when Justin buzzed again. "Christian from Marketing to see you."

All the warm feelings fled. "Send him in."

Zane sat back in his chair.

Christian shuffled in. The man was Zane's age, clean cut, good at his job. There were no outward signs that the man was a thief.

"Hey, Zane. You wanted to see me?"

"Sit, Christian." Zane steepled his hands. "I wanted to discuss the money you've been siphoning from my business accounts into your shell company."

The man froze.

Zane's gut burned, but he shoved the sensation down.

Ever since he'd first achieved some success, there had always been people looking for a handout, wanting a piece of what he'd worked hard for, risked things for.

And people who felt they could steal it.

He'd dealt with this before, and unfortunately he knew this wouldn't be the last. It just fucking stung when it was someone he trusted.

Christian went white. "I don't know—"

"Don't make this any worse by lying. The forensic accountant showed me the evidence this morning."

The man slumped into one of the guest chairs. "Zane, I was desperate. I'm sorry—"

Zane held up a hand, and Christian clamped his mouth shut.

"There are always plenty of excuses for making a poor decision. This one will cost you your job."

Tears appeared in Christian's eyes.

Zane blew out a breath, then pressed a button on the phone.

"Justin, send in my lawyers." He had no time for thieves. Everyone wanted something from him—his name, his money, his influence—never just him.

The lawyers appeared and Christian stood on shaky legs.

"I'm sorry."

Zane nodded. "I'll let you work things out with the lawyers. If you're lucky, we won't push for criminal charges."

He watched the man walk out with the lawyers, head hanging low.

Zane kept his mind off Christian as he sat through three more meetings. When he walked into the cavernous dining room at Eleven Madison Park, he needed a drink. A remorseful Christian had worked out a deal with the lawyers, and his desk had been cleared out.

They were always remorseful once they were caught.

He spotted Mav sitting at a table and crossed the restaurant to meet his friend.

A woman in a purple dress stepped in front of Zane, blocking his way.

"Hello." Her smile was slow, sensual.

Zane wasn't in the mood. "I'm meeting someone."

She held up a card, and slipped it in the pocket of his suit jacket.

"Call me." With a toss of her mane of brown hair, she strode off like she was on the catwalk at Fashion Week.

He watched her go and didn't feel a blip of interest.

He took out the card, and slipped it into a glass of melting ice on an uncleared table.

He pulled out the chair at Mav's table and sat.

"You look cheerful," Mav noted.

"Caught my marketing guy stealing. I haven't had the best morning."

Mav frowned. "Sorry, Zane."

"I'm sick of people fucking wanting a piece of me for their own selfish reasons." He shook his head. "I donate millions to charity to help people in need, but others, usually far less needy, think they're entitled to take it." He shook his head. "Let's not talk about it. How's your day?"

"Good. I've been busy with a search engine project."

"Tell me that my new safe got installed?"

"Yep. The guys told me it's all done."

"Thanks, Mav. I'm going to put my mom's necklace in there. She's coming down for her birthday in a few weeks."

"How's she doing?"

"Loves her new house in Westchester." Zane had bullied her until she'd chosen a nice place that he could buy for her.

Carol Roth was damn hard to spoil.

Others wanted to steal from him, but his own mom

rarely took what was offered until Zane coerced her into it.

A server brought over a bottle of wine, and lifted it for Mav's inspection. He nodded. "Thanks. Pour. My friend needs a drink."

"Hell yeah," Zane agreed.

Monroe

Ugh, these ugly, gray pants were way too tight.

I tugged at the waistband of my borrowed pants, then hefted my bucket of cleaning supplies and walked into the elevator.

I stood with the rest of the cleaning crew. There were five of us. Maria, the supervisor, eyed me skeptically.

The owner of Ivy Park Cleaning was a friend—who cleaned for many a wealthy person in Manhattan—and the woman owed me a favor. I'd changed the locks for her college-student daughter, and just after, a crazed ex-boyfriend had tried to attack the girl. My locks had prevented him from hurting her.

Today, I was going undercover as a cleaner. I'd scrub Zane Roth's bathroom, and scope out his place.

Perfect.

Unfortunately, the cleaning uniform was not comfortable, and my pants were one size too small. I also wore a blonde-brown wig that was itchy as hell.

The rest of the cleaning crew were talking quietly amongst themselves as the elevator finally slowed.

"You clean, and you do it well," the supervisor ordered. "Don't touch Mr. Roth's things, and stay in your assigned rooms."

We all nodded.

I'd been assigned the hallway, two guest rooms, and Roth's master bathroom and bedroom.

The hall would have easy access to his office. I had a small pin camera on my lapel and I'd start recording as soon as I entered. I needed all the layout information I could gather, so I could plan my breaking and entering.

My chest locked, but I made myself remember my brother. His life depended on me.

The elevator doors opened, and I stepped out. The breath rushed out of me and my mouth dropped open.

God, the place was stunning. The pictures of it hadn't done it full justice.

I would kill to live here.

"Get to work," Maria ordered.

We split up. I passed the sleek kitchen and drooled a little over the huge island and shiny appliances. I loved to bake, and baking here would be a dream. I gave the incredible view of Central Park a glance, rolled my eyes, and got to work.

I headed down the hall. Man, it really paid to have a squillion dollars.

My entire apartment would fit in one of these guest rooms. I picked up my cloth and bottle of cleaning spray.

I cleaned the guest room and bathroom. *Easy.* It looked like it hadn't been used recently. I glanced out the window. Even the guest room's ensuite had a nice view.

Peeking into the hall, I cocked my head. I heard a

vacuum cleaner somewhere. Slipping out, I moved quickly down the hall. My wig itched and I scratched my hairline.

I opened the doors along the hall. Another guest room. Sitting room. The next door was locked.

This had to be the office.

I quickly pulled my lock picks out of my pocket and set to work. The door clicked open.

Excellent. I couldn't deny the exciting little thrill.

I hated everything my father stood for, but I couldn't say I didn't understand what attracted him to his work.

As a little girl, I'd been his shadow. Before, when I was too young to understand that it was wrong, I'd had fun as he'd taught me to pick a lock, crack a safe, or pick-pocket some tourist in Times Square. I'd thought it was normal to know every safe on the market, and their strengths and weaknesses. I'd been proud when I'd crack a safe and my father would give me candy as a reward.

You're a chip off the ole block, Monny.

Suddenly, I heard footsteps. *Shit.* I pulled the door closed, spun and crouched down, pretending to clean the baseboards.

The eagle-eyed Maria appeared. I gave her a wide smile, then the woman walked down the hall and disappeared from view.

I kept dusting. I could hear Maria in the living room, and I waited until I was sure she was gone before I ducked into the office.

Right. I needed to get this done fast.

But before I could take any pictures, I heard the voices of two other cleaners getting closer.

Dammit.

I ducked back into the hall, and quickly disappeared into the next guest room. I got to work dusting, then cleaned the bathroom until it sparkled.

When I moved back into the hall, I saw another cleaner mopping the marble tile floors, and frustration hit me like a fist.

Shit. I still couldn't get back into the office. I wrestled with my frustration. Okay, I'd have to clean the master, and then try again after.

I opened the double doors at the end of the hall.

Oh, wow.

The room was long, and one side was all windows. The gorgeous bed had a blue-gray cover on it. A vase of cream flowers with a beautiful scent sat on the bedside table, and the carpet was plush underfoot. A chaise lounge near the windows urged someone to sit and read a book, if you could tear your gaze off the view.

I took a second to dream. The vacuum cleaner was just outside in the hall, droning on. There was an expensive-looking suit draped over a chair.

I walked into the bathroom.

Double wow.

The big, free-standing tub was set against the windows. Oh, yeah, people totally needed a view of Central Park while they soaked in the tub.

Hmm, the shower stall was still damp. I stepped closer, and then caught a glimpse of movement out of the corner of my eye. I spun.

Just as a billionaire strode out of the adjoining doorway.

A damp, very naked billionaire.

My brain short-circuited.

My cloth and bottle dropped out of my nerveless fingers and hit the marble tiles.

Zane Roth's head snapped up. Beautiful, hazel eyes met mine.

I took a step back...and slipped in a puddle of water. With a cry, my feet flew out from under me, and I was falling.

Roth lunged toward me, trying to grab me. My butt hit the tiles, and I looked up and found myself eye level with a long, beautiful, uncut cock.

Oh. *God.*

I scrambled back, heat in my cheeks.

"Are you okay?"

His voice was deep and masculine, and left goose bumps over my skin.

"I'm sorry. *So* sorry." I knew I should look away or cover my eyes, but my body wouldn't obey. Nope, my brain had gone on strike.

He had a sculpted chest, bronze skin, and abs. So many abs. Strong, toned legs, and had I mentioned the perfect cock? His scent hit me—freshly showered male, and something that made me think of the sea.

"I'm fine. You're fine. Very fine." *Shit. Pull it together, Monroe.* I scrambled to my feet. "You weren't supposed to be home." *Because I needed to scope out your home office so I could steal from you.*

He reached out and grabbed a towel off the rail and wrapped it around his hips. A faint smile danced around his mouth. His dark hair was damp, and I saw a bead of water roll down his pec, then lower—

"You sure you're okay?"

I blinked. "Yes. Sorry. I'm super sorry." I lifted my hand. "I'm here to...clean."

His lips twitched. "The uniform gave it away."

"Right." I sidled sideways. "I should..." *Work, brain.* "Go, and clean."

He bent down and grabbed the spray bottle and cloth. He handed them out to me. "I'm sorry I startled you."

"Right. Sure. Sorry for...seeing you naked." *Crap, stop talking, Monroe.*

The corner of Roth's eyes crinkled.

I took my things, and our fingers brushed. I felt a zap, like static electricity, and jerked.

My foot hit another patch of water and I slipped again.

Gasping, I reached out. My hand closed on Zane Roth's towel and my momentum yanked it off him. He stumbled.

I hit the tiles flat on my back...and a second later, a naked Zane Roth fell on top of me.

4

SHOWER-INTERRUPTING MINX

Zane

S hit. Naked and damp, Zane pressed his hands to the tiles. The sleek female body beneath him squirmed.

For the first time in a long time, a woman wasn't trying to get closer to him, she was trying to get away.

The woman pressed her hands to his shoulders, then jerked her hands away like he'd burned her.

"Hang on," he growled.

"*God.*" She turned her head to the side.

Her cheeks were pink, and she had ridiculously long lashes. Her brows and lashes were very black despite her golden-brown hair.

He pushed up and his foot slipped.

Fuck. He landed on her again, a set of small, firm breasts pressed against his bare chest. She grunted, and his cock pressed right between her legs.

"Get *off*," she said.

"I'm trying."

"What did you do to get all this water on the floor?" she snapped.

"I forgot my towel. Hence why you caught me naked."

"I didn't know you were here!"

"Really?"

Her head whipped around and eyes the color of thunderclouds met his. Their faces were only an inch apart.

Fuck, she had gorgeous gray eyes.

Her eyebrows rose. "You think I came in here, and slipped down, all so I could rub up against you?"

"Wouldn't be the first time a woman's tried something like that."

"Oh, well, boo-hoo, it must be tough being a gazillionaire with women throwing themselves at you all day long."

"It has its pros and cons."

"Off," she bit out through clenched teeth.

Zane carefully rose. The woman leaped up and nearly slipped again.

He grabbed her arm, and she pressed her hand over her eyes.

"Can you cover up, please?" She waved a hand at him.

He snatched up his lost towel and wrapped it around his hips. "That's not what women usually say to me."

Her hand dropped. "God, are you arrogant or what?"

She had a low, sexy voice.

"I'm just stating a fact. I'm decent by the way."

ANNA HACKETT

Her gaze dropped to his chest, then danced away. "You shouldn't walk around stark naked."

He raised a brow. The pretty blush on her cheeks was attractive, although her hair didn't suit her. "I shouldn't be naked in my own bathroom?"

The woman made a sound. "You weren't *supposed* to be here."

"You didn't hear the shower?"

"The vacuum was going."

"Well, I didn't expect to be attacked."

She glared at him. "I did *not* attack you."

"You dragged me to the floor, tore my towel off—"

She made an angry sound, and he wondered why he was having such a good time teasing her.

"Why, you—"

There was a squawk from the doorway. Maria, the cleaning supervisor, rushed in.

"Mr. Roth, I am so sorry." The woman grabbed his intruder's shoulder and dragged her out of the bathroom.

"Hey!" his attacker cried.

"Quiet. Out. Out now!"

His accidental attacker shot him a venomous look, then poked her tongue out.

Maria yanked her out of view.

Zane had the strangest reaction. He got hard.

Yep, his little shower-interrupting minx was the most fun he'd had in ages.

He stepped into his walk-in closet, and pulled on jeans and a dark-blue Henley. He hurried out to see Maria ushering her team of cleaners into the elevator.

She was still berating his wayward cleaner.

"You *never* disturb Mr. Roth."

"I didn't do it on purpose, trust me."

That deep, smoky voice hit him in all the right places. He wanted to know her name.

Then, the elevator doors closed, and they were gone.

Damn, he'd missed his chance.

With a shake of his head, Zane headed back to his bedroom.

That's when he noticed the door to his home office was ajar.

He frowned. The cleaning service had strict instructions not to disturb his office. And the door had been locked.

He often left confidential contracts and plans lying on his desk.

He pushed the door open. Light streamed in through the windows, and there was no sign that anything had been touched or disturbed.

Maybe he'd forgotten to lock it?

The Riv3000 was set low in the wall behind his desk. Its black, toughened door matched the shiny, black surface of his desk.

He walked over to the side table and grabbed himself a bottle of San Pellegrino from the mini fridge. Then he sat at his desk. He had work to do. His mother said he worked too hard, but his business didn't run itself, and he had lots of employees depending on him.

He opened his briefcase and pulled a black box out.

He sat the box on the desk and opened it.

The Phillips-Morley necklace gleamed up at him.

It was beautiful. A symbol of love.

Zane snorted. It was a good, solid investment that would put a smile on his mom's face.

That was it.

He turned to the safe, then pressed his finger to the scanner, and heard a discreet beep. He pressed in a code, and the door opened.

He set the necklace inside the safe and closed the door.

He sipped his water. Instead of work, he found himself thinking of enraged gray eyes, and he smiled.

Monroe

Lips traveled down my body, then across my bare stomach.

I moaned, writhing on the sheets.

"You like that, don't you?" a deep voice drawled. He nipped my skin, his teeth dragging over my inner thigh. "Your skin is so smooth."

I moaned. *So good.* I needed more.

That clever mouth closed over my clit.

I cried out, the pleasure so intense, and I slid my hands into that thick, brown hair. He licked and sucked, and a second later, I splintered apart with a shattered cry.

With a gasp, I sat up in my twisted sheets, my chest heaving, the orgasm still shivering through my body.

Oh, fuck a duck. I'd just had an X-rated dream about Zane Roth.

And had the best orgasm I'd had in years.

I flopped back on the pillows and stared at the ceiling. My thighs were sticky and my belly still warm and trembly. *Shit. Crap. Shit.*

Cursing under my breath, I glanced at the clock on the bedside table. It had been a gift from Sabrina, and she'd laughed herself silly when she'd given it to me. Instead of numbers on the clock face, it had stick people doing it in different sex positions. I squinted. It wasn't even doggy-style o'clock.

It was still early and I didn't have to open the shop for several hours, but I sure as hell wasn't going to lie in bed thinking about Zane Roth...and any sexual position, doggy style or other. I climbed out of bed and hit the bathroom.

Unlike Zane's massive bathroom, mine was compact and ordinary, with tiles that had probably been white in a previous life, but were now a sort-of dingy gray. Nothing like his sumptuous, palatial master bathroom with its giant shower, sexy tub, and awesome view. I instantly pictured us rolling around on the tiles of his bathroom, Roth gloriously naked.

I groaned and pressed my hands to my eyes.

Dropping my hands, I looked in the mirror. My black hair was spilling everywhere, my cheeks were flushed.

"We do *not* have sex dreams about billionaires, O'Connor. The daughters of criminals, about to commit crimes themselves, do not breathe the same air as sexy, hot billionaires."

I shed my pajamas and then got in my not-giant shower, and images of a naked Zane and his very fine cock danced in my head.

ANNA HACKETT

"Ugh." I turned the water to cold. "Ow. Ow. *Ow*." Okay, cold was sucky. I allowed myself lukewarm, and washed my hair.

When I was done, I dried off, ruthlessly suppressing X-rated billionaire thoughts.

God, my brother was in trouble, and here I was, thinking about a hot guy.

I wiped through the fog in the mirror and pulled my hair back in a tight ponytail. I dressed in my usual uniform of jeans, and my black and red Lady Locksmith polo shirt.

I needed to get back inside Zane's penthouse.

Pondering that, I headed into my kitchen. It was snug, but had been renovated not too long ago. It was mostly white, with a simple gray countertop. I poured myself some orange juice, then pulled out ingredients to make cookies. I needed them to bribe Rollo, plus I was the queen of stress-baking when I was anxious.

As I mixed the batter, I turned over my problem in my head. How to get back into Zane's penthouse? I dumped a bag of chocolate chunks into the bowl. I could feel the deadline Mag's captor had given me ticking down in my head.

Thankfully, baking helped. It didn't solve my problems, but as I placed the cookies on the tray, I felt a little more even. I stuck the tray in the oven.

Soon my apartment smelled like cookies. Who could feel depressed with the smell of cookies in the air? After my choc-chunk delights cooled, I packed them into a container. I had to open my shop, then later I'd visit Rollo.

After I opened, the shop got busy. I sold locks, recommended a safe, cut keys, and checked in with my team of locksmiths. Sabrina arrived and dived into serving customers. When it finally quieted down, I sat down to write my latest article on the best locks for windows.

I avoided Sabrina's latest wedding interrogation. Maybe I should call my ex, Joe, to go to the wedding with me? We were still on friendly terms. We'd had no real spark, but he was a nice guy.

Hell, dreams of Zane Roth had given me a better orgasm than Joe ever had.

Box of cookies in hand, I sailed through the store. "Sabrina, I'm heading out for a bit."

"I've got it."

Outside the shop, I unlocked my bike. I rode down the street, dodging traffic. Rollo lived in my neighborhood, so I didn't have far to go. I reached his place, locked up my bike, and walked down the steps to his basement apartment. I knocked on the door. Then knocked again.

"Go away," a voice said through the door.

"Rollo, it's Monroe."

There was a grunt and the door opened.

Rollo looked like a younger version of Doc Brown from the *Back to the Future* movies. Mag and I had loved that series as kids. Rollo's wispy, brown hair was a crazy halo around his head. His features were dominated by a high forehead, and large, brown eyes.

"Down payment." I held out the tub of cookies.

Rollo snatched it and tore open the lid. He wandered back into his studio apartment and I followed and closed the door.

I'd met Rollo in the alley beside Lady Locksmith. Back then, he'd been homeless and hungry.

I'd helped him out, and got him into a shelter. Eventually, once I'd learned of his computer skills, I'd helped him find a job, and get this apartment.

Wrinkling my nose, I wound my way through empty soda cans and chip packets. He needed a broom. Or a shovel.

He sat in front of his computer, munching on the cookies. He had multiple screens. His chair squeaked, and he stuffed another cookie in his mouth and chewed, crumbs flying everywhere.

"It wasn't easy getting schematics for the Riv3000, girly."

I perched on the edge of his desk, and felt a spike of anxiety. "Tell me you got them."

He shot me a look. "It was an *epic* hack. Rivera Tech has hella good security." Rollo blew on his fingers. "But they were no match for the Rollster."

I released a breath. "You got them."

"Yep." He tapped his keyboard and schematics flashed up on the screen.

"Oh, wow." My pulse spiked and I leaned forward, drinking in the design.

"It's got a keypad pin and biometric lock," Rollo said, tone impressed. "Plus the most complicated glass relockers I've ever seen."

My stomach plummeted. *Shit.* Maybe it *was* unbreakable. Glass relockers were panes of tempered glass set within the walls of a safe. If a thief tried to drill in and the glass broke, it triggered hardened relocker pins.

If you set off the glass relocker, then you were screwed. The only way into the safe was to cut it open.

"It's going to be popular." Rollo talked with his mouth full of cookie. "And expensive. Heard some rich dude here in New York got one of the first ones."

"Really?" I kept my voice bland.

"Yeah. He's having some fancy party tonight. For a bunch of rich people." Rollo's nose wrinkled. He said "rich people" the same way some would say "terrorists."

"A party?" *Hmm.*

"This safe's going to be a challenge to crack, girly, even for you."

"Can you and Bash make me a prototype?"

Bash was a friend of Rollo's—a welder and scrap-metal artist. The guy could make just about anything. He also had a kick-ass 3D printer.

Rollo sniffed. "When do I get my cheesecake?"

"When it's done," I replied.

"Fine, fine. I'll call Bash."

"Rollo, I need it tomorrow."

Rollo squeaked. "Girly, we're good, but not miracle workers."

"I'll make you two cheesecakes."

He huffed out a breath. "Fine."

I reached out and ruffled Rollo's hair. "Thanks, Rollo. You're a lifesaver." *Literally.*

Now all I needed to do was work out how to get another look at Zane Roth's home office.

And not his naked body.

Looked like I was going to crash a party.

5

PARTY-CRASHER

Monroe

My high heels clicked on the tiles of the lobby of Zane Roth's building. The short hem of my dress flirted with my upper thighs. It was several steps up from my tight cleaning uniform.

I saw several well-dressed guests ahead of me. Men in well-cut suits, and women in short, designer dresses.

They were showing invites to a guard situated near the elevator. I sidled closer and fluffed my sleek, platinum-blonde wig. It was a sharp bob that ended at my jaw line. The dress had cost me an eye-watering amount. I'd stuck it on my already overloaded credit card. It was emerald-green, and essentially had no back except for some tiny straps. I'd done dramatic eyes, and was wearing killer black stilettos. Killer because they were already killing my feet.

I should fit right in.

I moved close to the back of one suit-clad man in

front of me. Like we were a couple. The guard looked at the man's invite, nodded at me, before his gaze drifted down my legs.

Excellent.

I stood in the back corner of the elevator. The other guests were chatting, talking about someone's upcoming socialite wedding.

"Drusilla still can't decide on the flowers."

"I heard the budget for the flowers alone was eighty thousand."

My eyes popped wide. Eighty grand on flowers?

"I heard Roth's place is *fabulous*," a woman drawled. "Bought it for sixty-six million."

I almost choked. *Sixty-six million? Jeez.*

The elevator slowed and the doors opened.

Music came through hidden speakers and people were dotted around the spacious living area. White-uniformed servers with trays moved among the crowd with drinks and canapés.

I didn't drink much. My dad had been a heavy drinker, and I'd learned early on that I needed to stay sharp.

"Drink, miss?" A server with a tray full of flutes of champagne stopped beside me.

"Oh, I don't think so."

"It's Dom Pérignon."

Well, what the hell? It might help settle my jangling nerves. "Thank you."

I took a flute, then wandered the edges of the party, circling closer to the corridor leading to Roth's office.

My plan was to blend into the party, slip into his

office, take my photos, and get out.

I sipped the champagne. *Oh, boy.* I stifled a moan. The bubbles tickled my tongue. *Mmm, nectar of the gods.*

I followed the flow of partygoers upstairs to the terrace. I turned and my heart took a giant leap into my throat.

Zane was out by the railing, the darkness of Central Park behind him. He wore charcoal pants, and a white shirt that was fitted to his toned body. A hank of dark hair fell over his forehead and my gaze drifted along that strong jaw.

He was nodding at someone. Damn him for being so gorgeous. And larger-than-life. He exuded power, and made a woman imagine all kinds of things she shouldn't be imagining.

I stepped closer, studying him more intently. His handsome face had a look on it, almost bored. He looked removed from the party around him.

I gave a mental snort. *Right.* Poor rich billionaire bored at his fancy party in his multimillion-dollar penthouse.

I lifted the flute, tipped it, and drank it all. Pleasant heat hit my belly.

"Not enjoying yourself?" a deep voice with a British accent asked.

I spun.

Instantly, I recognized the man. Another billionaire bachelor—Liam Kensington.

He was too handsome for words, but where Zane had dark-brown hair, Liam's was burnished-blond. Like polished gold. He had a narrower face and blue eyes.

"Oh, no, it's a great party. I just...it's been a long day."

"You've had a rough day? I sympathize."

"Hmm." I really didn't need Zane Roth's best friend noticing me.

"I don't believe we've met." His blue eyes held an appreciative gleam.

"No, I don't often hang out with billionaires."

Kensington raised a brow. "Despite the worth of our companies, we still eat, sleep, and breathe."

"Right." I made a point of scanning the plush terrace area. I glanced at Zane again. He lifted his head and looked my way. *Crap.* I quickly spun, giving him my back.

Liam's lips quirked. "Do you have a problem with rich people?"

"Well, they're just so...rich."

He laughed. "You're quite refreshing, Miss...?"

I smiled back and just raised a brow.

"Ms. Mystery, then." He cocked his head. "How do you know Zane?"

"Oh, a friend of a friend. I don't really know him that well."

"Really?" Liam looked over my shoulder. "Because he's coming this way."

I barely swallowed a squeak. "Great. But first I need another drink." I turned.

"I can get you one," Liam offered.

"No, it's fine." I pushed deeper into the crowd, and away from Liam Kensington and Zane Roth, or any other person with lots and lots of zeros at the end of their bank accounts.

I needed to get into that office. *Now*.

I heard a burst of laughter from a group nearby and circled around them. Then I bumped into a hard chest.

"*Oof.*" I looked up.

Jesus, it was the final billionaire bachelor—Maverick Rivera. God, what was with me attracting all these billionaires today?

Rivera was too rugged to be called handsome. He had a heavy scruff, bronze skin, and was attractive in a rough kind of way. He was also the inventor of the Riv3000.

"Sorry," I said.

The man scowled. "You should watch where you're going."

I kind of liked his surly attitude. "And you shouldn't take up so much room." I sidestepped around him.

Man, I'd gone my whole life never meeting a billionaire, now here I was running into them all over the place.

I headed down the stairs and hurried down the hall. I passed a couple kissing. Wow, they were really going at it.

Moving past them, I paused. I took out my lock pick from my tiny handbag, quickly opened the door, and slipped in.

It was dark in the office, with only the city lights filtering in through the windows.

I turned on a lamp on the desk.

My camera was embedded in the pendant on my necklace. I lifted it and started taking shots. The door, the furniture, and the safe.

It was set in the wall and looked so unassuming.

I leaned in close to get several more shots of it.

Then I glanced around, and took shots of the

window, the ceilings, the air vents, the walls.

Finally, I turned and stared at the safe.

"I'll get you to sing for me." My fingers itched. I did love a challenge.

I heard laughter in the hall. *Crap*. I needed to go.

I turned off the light and opened the door, quickly sliding into the hall. Then I hurried back toward the living room.

Right. Get through the party and get out of here.

I turned a corner and slammed into a hard chest.

This chest was covered in a snowy-white shirt. A fabulous cologne that reminded me of the sea hit my senses.

Uh-oh.

"Are you okay?" a deep voice asked.

I looked up into familiar hazel eyes.

***

Zane

Zane had been searching the party for another tantalizing glimpse of the woman in the tiny, green dress.

He was trying to find a distraction to get the big, gray eyes of his bathroom attacker out of his head.

A woman came out of the hall and collided with him. He grabbed her elbows.

"Are you okay?" he asked.

She looked up. Large, gray eyes widened.

"*You*," he breathed. Was he dreaming? Hallucinating?

Her hair was different, and he wasn't sure the sleek, silver-blonde suited her any better.

"Um…"

"You snuck back into my place?"

Her gaze never looked away from him, bold, direct. "Yes?"

"You asking me, or telling me?"

She straightened, a spark in her eyes. "Well, obviously I'm here."

He slid his hands up her toned arms. She was tall, long, and sleek.

Zane lowered his voice. "Couldn't stop thinking about me?"

She cocked her head. "That is so arrogant. You think if someone sees you, then they can't stop thinking about you. Dreaming about you."

He grinned, feeling a sharp bite of excitement. "I never said anything about dreaming." He lowered his head and heard her breath hitch. "Have you been dreaming about me since you stripped me naked and knocked me over?"

She sucked in a breath. "I didn't…" There was a struggle for control on her face. "I didn't dream about you."

He stared at her pink cheeks. "Liar."

"I didn't!" she whisper-yelled.

"You are a really bad liar."

"Actually, I'm a pretty good liar."

Someone bumped into them and Zane lifted his head. It was a business associate who Zane had been purposely avoiding.

The man smiled, showing a mouthful of perfect veneers. "Oh, hey, Roth, I wanted to talk to you about—"

"Not now." Zane took his mystery woman's hand and dragged her away.

"Hey, that was rude," she said.

"It's a party, and he was about to be rude. He was going to ask me for a loan."

She was quiet for a moment. "That is rude."

"There are people clamoring for a minute of my time every day. Asking for money every day."

"Hmm, I guess it's rough being insanely wealthy." She spoke in a deadpan voice.

Zane fought back a smile. He liked this sassy woman —who didn't simper, tell him what she thought he wanted to hear.

He pulled her up the stairs and onto the terrace. He tugged her away from the guests standing by the door and pulled her to a quiet, shadowed spot by the railing. It had a great view of the city and the park, and he often stood here when he needed to clear his head.

She turned to take in the view, but Zane was too busy looking at her.

She was beautiful, but not in a conventional way. She didn't have that careful, plucked-and-pruned look like many of the women inside. She had high cheekbones, long lashes, and those fascinating, cloud-gray eyes.

"I want to know your name," he said.

She dragged her gaze off the view and cocked her hip. "Well, we don't always get what we want."

"I do."

"It's good for the soul to hear no sometimes, Roth."

"Is that a rule?"

She shot him a hot look and he felt it in his cock.

A group of people nearby laughed and she turned her head. "You're missing out on your party. You should be over there, talking to your friends."

"Most of these people are acquaintances, at best." He shrugged a shoulder. "Hell, a lot of them annoy me."

She cocked her head. "By asking you for money?"

Zane nodded. "Or a meeting, an introduction to someone, or backing for their amazing project. They want to shortcut the line and get an easy pass, usually off the back of my hard work."

"Hard work? Don't you billionaires just sit around in your plush corner offices and sip champagne all day? Or go sailing, or something?"

"Ha-ha."

"I imagine it takes a lot of hard work to keep an empire like yours running."

"It does."

Something moved through her gray eyes. "Well, don't worry, I'm not going to ask you for money." Her teeth flashed. "Of course, if you have a spare million lying around and you don't know what to do with it..."

He laughed. A server passed by with a tray of canapés. Zane waved a hand and his mystery woman snagged one. She eyed the small piece of baguette topped with crème fraîche and a dollop of orange.

With a shrug, she popped it in her mouth. Her body locked, and she quickly held her napkin up and spat. "Oh, God, what is that? It's disgusting."

"Sea urchin."

Her nose wrinkled. She walked over to a table and dumped the napkin on a discarded plate. "Well, I know one place where you can spend some of your money. On tastier food."

Delighted with her, he just stared. When was the last time a woman had spat food out in front of him and didn't feel an ounce of self-consciousness?

She leaned back against the railing. "So why throw a fancy party at your fancy penthouse if you don't want to spend time with all these people?"

Shit, it was a good question. "I don't know, it's expected? I guess I like some of them in small doses."

"Do you have any good friends? Ones you laugh with, who have your back, who annoy you for good reasons?"

"I'm pretty damn lucky to have a couple. Liam and Mav."

"Never heard of them." She kept a straight face, but her lips twitched.

Zane grinned. "They give me shit, don't let me get away with much, and yes, they have my back." He paused. "You have friends like that?"

She lifted a slim shoulder and he tried not to get distracted by her pale skin. "One or two. One who's a pain in my ass, mostly, but I love her. She doesn't let me get away with *anything*, and she nags like a pro. But other than that, I'm too busy working to have time to make friends."

"As a cleaner."

She made a humming noise.

"What about family?" he asked. "They have your

back?"

She stiffened. "Not so much."

Zane could practically see the "steer clear" signals on this topic, and didn't want to upset her. "Sorry, I—"

"Mostly my family make my life harder, not easier," she said quietly.

His chest tightened. "Your parents?"

"I never knew my mom. She left when I was little. And my father...let's just say he's never going to win father of the year."

Zane felt a tug of kinship. "Mine either. He abandoned me and my mom when I was seven."

His mystery blonde's face softened. "I'm sorry. It isn't easy being alone."

"I wasn't. My mom is great."

"You're lucky."

He wondered if she had ever been lucky. With no mother, and a less-than-stellar father, who'd cared for her, provided for her, taught her all the things kids needed to learn?

Then she turned away, and Zane's body locked. Her dress barely had any back. Just a few crisscrosses of thin straps. His gaze traced over delicate shoulder blades, smooth skin. Yet there was nothing delicate about this woman. She had a strength to her.

Something made him think his mystery woman was a survivor. She'd face whatever life tossed at her with an eye-roll and a curse.

His gaze dropped lower. She was lean, but had a gorgeous ass.

He pressed closer, touching a hand to her shoulder.

She tensed, but didn't push him away.

He ran his fingers down her skin and she shivered. He leaned in, his lips brushing her ear as his fingers traced her spine.

"Tell me your name. Please."

"Tiffany."

He snorted. "It is not."

"Barbie."

He didn't dignify that with an answer.

"Brittany."

He spun her and their gazes locked.

"Tell me." He ran his fingers along her jaw.

Her ridiculously long eyelashes fluttered. "Monroe." She jerked. "Shit, no, it isn't. It's Monique."

His gut hardened. *Finally*. "Monroe." It suited her. "Why are you here?"

She sighed. "It's complicated."

"It always is."

"There's a guy."

Zane's body reacted at the thought of another man. "A lover?"

"What? No, he's—" She clamped her mouth shut.

"Complicated?" Zane slid a hand around the back of her neck. No cloying perfume for Monroe. She smelled like fresh soap, with a faint tang of citrus.

She leaned into him. "I have to go."

"No, you don't." His mouth was a whisper from hers. He saw desire in her eyes. "I want you to stay."

"I'm no good for you, Zane Roth, trust me."

"Let me be the judge of that."

He pressed his mouth to hers.

6

NO GOOD CHOICES

Monroe

Oh, God.

O I'd been fighting the pull of him since he'd found me—his gorgeous scent, the feel of his body, the pure, masculine power radiating off him.

But those firm lips on mine sent every thought scattering out of my head.

I slid my hands up to cup his handsome face. Our mouths locked together and his tongue boldly stroked mine—deep and possessive.

My back hit the railing, and every bit of air left my lungs. I pressed closer, and his hands closed on my butt.

"This ass." It was a growl against my lips. "This perfect, curvy ass."

I moaned and bit his bottom lip. Then our mouths clashed again, melding hotly, a deep and drugging exploration.

My body vibrated with need.

His mouth slid down my neck, nipping, and making me shudder against his hard body. "*Yes.*"

"You like that?" He kissed me again. His mouth was bolder this time, his tongue stroking mine urgently.

I leaned into him, hunger blooming—hot and desperate—inside me. Here, right here in this man's arms, I felt things I'd never felt before.

Zane gripped my jaw, tilting my head, his kiss deepening and taking on a possessive edge that made my pulse skitter.

Suddenly, laughter broke out nearby, followed by the clink of glassware.

I jerked back, panting.

"Stay," he said. "I'll tell everyone to leave."

His voice was a growl, and I heard the hungry edge. Pure temptation.

This was a man who could get anything and anyone he wanted. If he knew who I truly was, he wouldn't want me.

"I can't."

Frustration twisted his features. "Why did you come here?"

I found it hard to fight through the fog of need. I dragged in a breath, and his gaze dropped to my chest. Desire was stark on his face.

I made myself think of Maguire. Guilt flooded me. He was a prisoner, and here I was kissing a billionaire.

I pushed Zane back a step.

"Monroe?"

More guilt tipped over me. I was lying to him. I was planning to steal from him.

Turning my head, I fought the helpless anger. I hated having no good choices.

A finger nudged my chin and his hazel eyes met mine —intelligent, penetrating.

I grabbed his wrist. "I...I have to go."

His fingers tightened on my chin, then he nodded. "Give me your number? Please."

I nodded. It was the quickest way to get out of here. He pulled a pen out of his pocket and I steeled myself, then lied again.

I wrote a bogus number on his wrist.

When I pulled away, he grabbed my arm. Quickly, he wrote his number on my forearm. "Monroe—"

My belly contracted and I turned away. If I stayed any longer, I'd give in to the temptation.

I looked back. He stood there on the terrace, the cool, night breeze blowing his thick hair, his shirt tucked into the narrow waist. There was strength under those tailored clothes. I'd felt it.

"I'm sorry." I had to hurt him, use him, and take a piece of what was his.

Just like everyone tried to do.

He frowned and stepped toward me.

I turned and ran.

I rushed back inside and shoved through the party guests. God, my hands were shaking.

When I made it to the elevator, I stabbed the button. When the doors opened, I stepped inside, sure he'd catch me. The doors closed, and I sagged against the wall.

I'd gotten my photos. My stomach churned.

And I'd kissed Zane Roth.

Desire still fluttered through me, and I reached up and touched my lips. *God.* I should never have let him see me.

He'd wonder why I was here. Again.

And I'd told him my name. *Idiot.*

I blew out a breath and pressed my palms against the wall. At least I hadn't told him my surname. Once the necklace was gone, there was no way he'd ever trace it to me.

The elevator stopped, and I half ran out into the lobby.

"Good night, miss."

I managed a nod to the doorman before I burst outside.

I strode down the street at a fast clip. Around the corner, I yanked the wig off my head, my real hair falling loose.

Pausing, I glanced up at the tall, slender tower that housed Zane's home. "I'm so sorry."

Then I set my shoulders back. Mag's life depended on me getting the necklace.

Zane Roth would recover. He'd forget about the woman he'd kissed on a balcony. He was probably kissing another woman right now.

The thought felt like claws in my belly.

I flagged down a cab and climbed in. After I'd given the driver my address, I leaned back and closed my eyes.

No more intimate *tête-à-têtes* with Zane Roth. I needed to steer clear.

What I really needed was a way to crack his safe. I'd

get in, steal the necklace, then get out. Then I'd get Mag home safely, and life would get back to normal.

A life where I didn't run into billionaires, and I certainly didn't kiss them.

Of course, I'd be a criminal, just like my father.

The thought was like black oil on my skin.

Zane would come nowhere near me, if he knew everything about me.

I really am sorry. I touched my lips again and fought back the surprising burst of pain.

Zane

Zane leaned on the railing, feeling a strange sense of loss.

He should never have let her leave.

Here he was, ignoring his guests, although he didn't miss the banter and inane conversations. He knew several of them were lurking, wanting his time to get advice, or ask for money.

They never wanted him.

He looked at the number scrawled on his wrist in bold writing. He lifted his cell and dialed her number.

"Anthony's Pizza."

Zane's gut curdled. "Is Monroe there?"

"Don't know a Monroe, man. You must have the wrong number. Got pies to make." The man hung up.

Dammit. Zane ground his teeth together. She'd lied to him.

She'd slipped through his fingers again.

"He looks far too solemn for a guy who was kissing a gorgeous woman only moments ago."

Liam leaned on the railing to Zane's left, one brow arched.

Mav appeared on his right. "Can we kick the guests out yet? Then we can open a good bottle of Scotch."

Liam studied Zane's face. He always was a perceptive bastard. It made him good at his work.

"I spotted the sexy woman in green first," Liam said.

An ugly sensation crawled through Zane's gut. "No, you didn't."

"I didn't make a move. Don't worry."

Zane's fingers curled into a fist. The numbers on his wrist mocked him. "I don't know who the hell she is."

Mav frowned. "Really?"

"It's the second time we've run into each other."

"A beautiful mystery lady who wasn't keen to stay and drink your champagne, fawn all over you, and tumble into your bed?" Liam mused. "Interesting."

"I'm going to find her," Zane said.

"Uh-oh," Mav muttered.

A smile curled Liam's mouth. "Someone's sounding a little infatuated."

Zane's head whipped up. "Fuck you."

"Definitely infatuated," Mav agreed.

"Intrigued," Zane countered.

Liam shifted. "Both start with I."

"Don't lose your head over a pretty face and a gorgeous set of legs," Mav warned.

Mav had been burned in college by a pretty woman who had been after his money.

"There's something about her..." Zane tapped his fingers on the railing. She was definitely hiding something. "She was on my cleaning crew the other day."

Liam's brows drew together. "And tonight she snuck into your party?"

"Alarm bells are ringing, Z," Mav said.

"I'm going to get the full story from her." Those gray eyes and sharp cheekbones appeared in his head.

She'd dreamed of him. His lips curved. He couldn't get her out of his mind.

She'd come for him. Heat filled his gut.

He was going to track her down, and he wasn't going to let her run again.

It took another hour, but finally, the party wound down. Then it was just him, Liam, and Mav.

They opened a bottle of Lagavulin, and Zane handed glasses to his friends.

"I need to go soon." Liam leaned back in an armchair. "I've got an early meeting at our latest construction site downtown."

"And I'm working at the tech lab tomorrow." Mav swirled his Scotch. "That way I can avoid as many boring meetings as I can."

"Howton chasing you to invest?" Zane asked.

"Every fucking day."

"Kensington, I saw an article about your impending engagement to Fernanda Alende," Zane said, referencing the statuesque, Brazilian supermodel.

Liam scowled. "I met her once. She was handsy, and always posing anytime a camera was around."

"And looking to snag a billionaire husband," Mav said darkly.

"Things were easier before we became successful and rich," Zane said, quietly.

"People were...real," Liam noted.

"Everyone wants a piece of us now." Mav knocked back his drink. "I'm taking my brooding ass home to bed." He rose.

Liam stood too. "We'll let Zane dream of sexy blondes in green dresses."

He shot his friends a look. "Bye, assholes."

Finally, he was alone. He wandered through the empty penthouse. The cleaners would come in the morning to tidy up.

He headed down the hall to his office and froze.

The door was unlocked again.

He scanned the shadowed room.

Someone had been in here. He circled the desk. It looked undisturbed. He glanced at his new Riv 3000 and it looked as shiny as ever.

He took a deep breath.

A scent hit him. *Soap.* With an undertone of citrus.

Monroe.

She'd been in here.

It's complicated.

A ball of lead hit Zane's gut. She was after something. He recognized that look he'd seen on her face now.

Guilt. Distress.

Fuck. He ran his hands through his hair and dropped into his desk chair.

She hadn't been here for him.

She was just another user on the take.

He looked at his Rolex, anger flaring inside him. It was late, but not too late on the West Coast.

He grabbed his desk phone and dialed.

A moment later a deep voice answered. "Norcross."

"Hi, Vander, it's Zane."

Vander Norcross was the head of Norcross Security. He was former military, and after a covert career on a Ghost Ops special-forces team, he'd gotten out and started his own private investigations and security company in San Francisco. He did a lot of work for Roth Enterprises.

"I need you to track someone down," Zane said.

"Go on."

"A woman. First name, Monroe. About five-foot-eight, gray eyes, and I think blonde hair. She snuck in with my cleaners the other day, and tonight, she crashed a party at my place."

"Not much to go on."

"She was in my home office." He looked at the numbers on his arm. "I don't know who the hell she is, or what she's after, but I want to find out."

"I'm on it," Vander replied.

And when Vander Norcross said he was on it, it meant he'd get the job done.

For a second, Zane relived that kiss, Monroe's body pressed against him. Then he squelched the memory.

He wouldn't let anyone play him for a fool.

7

TICK-TOCK

Monroe

The pounding on the front door of Lady Locksmith the next morning made me jerk. I jumped up from my desk and raced into the shop. We weren't open yet, so I had no idea who it was.

Through the glass, I saw Rollo's cloud of crazy hair. He had a huge cardboard box in his arms. He jerked his head at me.

I opened the door. "Hey."

Rollo grunted and pushed inside. He blinked at the light, his brown eyes scrunched. He reminded me of a mole coming into the sunlight.

"Where do you want this? Bash and I stayed up all night to get your prototype ready."

They'd done it. My heart skipped a beat. "Rollo, you are *amazing*. Put it on my desk." I hurried into the office and swiped the detritus off my desk.

Rollo set the box down. I got a better look at him now.

His eyes were bloodshot and he looked jittery—probably from too many of the energy drinks he loved.

"Did you sleep at all?" I asked.

"Hell, no. We were busy with this." He yawned so hard I thought I'd hear his jaw crack. "Bash is crashed out on my couch." Rollo reached into the box and hefted out the safe prototype.

Wow. I circled the prototype. It wasn't as pretty or as glossy as the one in Zane's office, but it had all the right bits in the right places, thanks to the schematics. It looked more like a skeleton of a safe, but I was most interested in the locking mechanisms.

My throat tightened. Rollo and Bash had definitely come through. I needed to get baking.

I turned to Rollo. "You came through for me." I felt a burn of tears in my eyes. God, I was really tired.

Rollo frowned at me. "You're not springing a leak are you?"

I swiped my arm across my face and sniffed. "No."

He looked alarmed. "Good...good." A pause. "You sure?"

"I'm sure. It's just been a rough few days."

He patted me awkwardly on the shoulder. "You want to...uh, talk about it?"

"No."

He blew out a breath. "Good. You got any more cookies?"

A laugh bubbled out of me. "No, but I have some cupcakes. I'll warn you, they're a few days old and probably a bit stale."

He grunted. "I don't care, I'll take 'em."

I raced up to my apartment and brought the cupcakes down. I handed them over and watched him sniff them. Bliss crossed his face.

"Thanks, Rollo."

"I'll be waiting for my cheesecakes." He headed out into the shop. He paused. "Good luck with the Riv3000."

I nodded.

He hesitated, then shifted his feet. "Uh, take care."

God, I must look bad. Warmth hit me in the chest. "You going soft on me, Rollo?"

"Fuck, no." He stuffed a cupcake in his mouth and headed out the door.

I locked it behind him.

As I headed back to my office, I yawned. I was so tired. After the party, I'd been too churned up to sleep.

After kissing Zane.

God, I'd kissed Zane Roth. I slapped a hand against my forehead.

And I'd loved every second of it.

I wanted more.

Stop thinking about him. I slumped against my desk. I was going to steal a necklace worth two million dollars from the man. Guilt made it hard to breathe.

My phone dinged.

It was a text message. I thumbed the screen and froze. It was a photo of Mag, gagged and tied to a chair.

Tick-tock.

Oh, God. Hot nausea washed over me. I didn't want to steal from Zane, but Maguire's life was at stake. I couldn't afford to be distracted by Zane's sexy body and hazel eyes.

With a deep breath, I turned back to the safe prototype and got to work. I braided my hair back to keep it out of my way and studied the parts.

It was like getting to know someone—their strengths, weaknesses, quirks. I could almost hear my father's voice, touched with a little Irish lilt even though he'd never stepped foot in Ireland. I'd grown up sitting at his knee, fiddling with safe parts, watching him work.

I'd been his willing student and offsider until I'd turned fourteen. Then I'd seen up close and personal the devastation his cons caused.

Stomach churning, I got to work. When I got up to make a cup of tea and stretch out the kinks in my neck, I grabbed my phone and made a few calls. For the information I needed, I'd have to pay in more than cookies or cupcakes. I could already hear my credit card weeping.

I dialed a number.

"Yeah?" a deep, rusty voice said.

"It's Monroe." I grabbed a mug from the shelf and dropped a tea bag into it.

A sound like a snort. "Been a while."

"I know, I'm surprised you're still alive," I told the aging private investigator. He was an old friend of my father's, and had done a few jobs for me here and there.

"Watch that smart mouth, kid."

"I need a work up on a woman. Monica Gorman." I poured hot water into the mug.

"Gorman?"

"Yes, I need her schedule." I rattled off the woman's address. "Her schedule in detail, and I need it by tomorrow."

"That doesn't come cheap, O'Connor," the voice rasped.

"Mac, this isn't my first rodeo."

Patrick "Mac" MacGee sniffed. "Money in my account first, then I'll start the job."

Some things never changed. I felt a headache starting behind my eyes. "Sure thing, Mac. Thanks."

The crusty old man hung up.

Rubbing my temple, I looked back at the safe. I sat down again, sipped my tea, and got back to work.

I wasn't sure how much time had passed before I heard the shop door open.

"Monroe!"

Sabrina. I rose, stretched, went to the office door. "Morning."

My friend's smile died. "You look even more tired today."

"Late night."

Sabrina perked up, and shoved a Starbucks coffee cup at me. "A date?"

"A party." I sipped the mocha and moaned. Sweet, sweet caffeine.

Sabrina pouted. "You went to a party without me?"

"It was last minute. No one you know. And you're an old, engaged woman now."

My friend wagged her finger, then settled in behind the counter. "Bite your tongue. Besides, we'll be partying tonight."

I blinked.

Sabrina's gaze narrowed. "You'd better not have forgotten my bachelorette party, Monroe."

Shit. "I haven't."

Sabrina made an annoyed sound. "I've known you long enough to know when you're lying, even though your damn good at it."

I had forgotten. I'd been too worried about Maguire. Shit, time was running out, but I couldn't let Sabrina down. I still had more work to do on the safe, and I wasn't quite ready to break into Zane's place, yet.

I shoved my guilt down, but it clung like mud.

"I'll be the life of the party tonight," I promised. "I remember we're heading to some new club. No strippers. I haven't forgotten." I went over and hugged my best friend. "You're marrying a good guy and I'm happy for you, babe."

Sabrina hugged her back. "I wish you could find a good one."

A handsome face flashed into my head. "Maybe one day."

"Well, let's at least start with a date for my wedding." Sabrina waved a hand. "Anyway, Mayfair is the hottest new club in the city."

"Cool." I tried to dredge up some excitement.

"It's owned by Liam Kensington."

Shit. I was tripping over billionaires everywhere. "The billionaire?"

"One of New York's billionaire bachelors." Sabrina shivered and let out a dramatic sigh. "We might run into him and his friends."

I was mid-sip of my coffee and scalded my tongue. "*What?*"

"Although, probably not," Sabrina said. "They had

some fancy party at Zane Roth's amazing penthouse on Billionaire's Row last night."

The coffee went down the wrong way and I coughed. "Oh?"

"Look at them." Sabrina slapped a newspaper on the counter. The front picture showed Zane, flanked by Liam and Maverick. Liam was smiling, Zane had a half grin on his face, and Maverick was scowling.

"They are *so* gorgeous. I'd take Zane." A dreamy look crossed Sabrina's face. "Or maybe Liam."

"Poor Andrew."

"My snookums knows I love him...unless a hot billionaire comes knocking." Sabrina grinned. "It does look like Zane might be taken."

My heart rammed against my ribs like a heavyweight boxer. "Really?"

Sabrina tapped a finger against the paper. There was a smaller picture of Zane at his party, out on the terrace. He was in profile...with a blonde in a green dress pressed against the railing.

Oh. *God.*

No one could tell it was me, but a part of me waited for Sabrina to recognize me.

"Lucky lady," Sabrina sighed.

I made a noncommittal noise, but I couldn't look away. The two of us looked so...sexy. He was cupping my face, all that intensity focused on me. Heat pooled in my belly.

"I have some work to do in the office," I mumbled.

"Go, I've got this." Sabrina put her hands on her hips. "I'm going to rearrange the window lock display."

In the privacy of my office, I got back to work on the safe. I tested a few things. I studied its innards from all angles. Tapping a finger against my lips, I worked it all through in my head. I almost had a plan worked out. I'd need to practice, multiple times, to be sure.

Now I just needed a way into Zane's home.

Horrible guilt closed my throat. I opened the desk drawer and looked down. It held the slip of paper that I'd written his number on, before I'd washed my arm.

I fingered it.

Then I pulled out a burner phone that I'd purchased with cash. Without letting myself think too hard, I dialed.

"Roth." His voice was deep, authoritative.

My pulse spiked. I hadn't actually expected him to answer. "Zane."

Silence. "You gave me a fake number, Monroe."

"Yes."

"I didn't expect to hear from you." His voice was hard. "You'd been in my office."

Oh, God, how did he know? "Zane—"

"I know a con when I see one." The harsh angry tone of his voice made my insides shrivel. "You're planning to steal from me."

I felt sick. "You don't understand."

"I understand *perfectly*. You're just another user. The world's full of them."

My hand curled around the phone. He sounded furious and I hated it. "Za—"

He hung up.

Slowly, I set the phone down, my heart hurting.

I couldn't blame him. It was exactly what I deserved.

Zane

The last place Zane wanted to be on a Saturday night was at Liam's newest club.

Music was pumping, and the place was packed. Or at least it was in the VIP area. He was up on the VIP mezzanine, and he looked down over the railing. No, it was packed below, as well. The dance floor was heaving.

Liam had decorated his new club like an English manor. There was a curved ceiling, elegant chandeliers, framed portraits and landscapes and a shiny, mahogany bar.

"A drink, sir?"

A polite, well-dressed server stood nearby.

"Scotch. Macallan."

The woman nodded.

Maverick arrived, leaning against the railing. "I did not want to come out tonight."

"You have to be social sometimes, Mav. Talk to flesh-and-blood people, not just computers or your inventions."

"Why?"

"So you don't become antisocial, with the personality of a rock."

Mav grunted.

Zane glanced over and saw Liam schmoozing with some others at the tables. A woman in a gold dress was clinging to him, leaning in and smiling like he knew the answer to the meaning of life.

"God, he enjoys the whole king-of-his-domain thing," Mav said.

"Must be his English blood."

The server brought Zane his drink. He sipped and enjoyed the burn.

"Any luck with your mystery blonde?" Mav asked.

"I have Vander tracking her down."

"Norcross? You called in the big guns."

"She'd been in my office. I'm pretty sure she's after something."

"Shit. Corporate espionage?"

"Could be." Zane couldn't stop thinking about those damn gray eyes. "Vander called an hour ago. He has a short list and should have a name soon."

"You've got everything important in your safe, right?"

Zane nodded. "And it's unbreakable."

"Hell, yeah."

Liam joined them. "Having fun?"

"Nice place," Mav said. "Can I go home now?"

"No." Liam shook his head. "I'm going to make you have some fun. You can't play with your gadgets all day."

"The club's great, Liam," Zane said. "Business seems brisk."

"Thanks. First week's earnings are exceeding expectations." Liam cocked his head. "What's wrong?"

Mav leaned forward. "His mystery woman likely wants to steal from him. She was casing his place, not him."

"Ouch." Liam's face turned serious. "You need help?"

"No." Zane shook his head. "I have Vander tracking her down. She isn't going to get away with anything."

Fury bubbled through him, and some other emotions he didn't want to analyze. He barely knew Monroe. Her betrayal shouldn't sting so much.

"Well, drink up. Try to have some fun." Liam nodded to a woman in a blue dress. "Tiffany asked to meet you."

The name made Zane choke back a laugh. "I can meet women on my own, Kensington."

"She might covet your money, but she won't steal it."

Zane shook his head.

Back at the railing, he peered at the throng below, and his gaze caught on a woman sporting a veil. A bachelorette party.

But his vision blurred, and it was Monroe's face that dominated his thoughts. Her body, her scent.

Fuck. He had to get her out of his mind.

His phone rang. He looked down at the screen. No number listed. He shouldn't answer.

Shit. He stabbed the button. "Roth."

All he could hear was the thump of music.

"I'm sorry."

At the sound of her voice, he gripped the phone. "About being a crap person?"

He heard her blow out a breath. "I'm not. It's..."

"Complicated," he responded sarcastically.

"It's easy to judge when you're rich, and you have everything you need and want. When you aren't helpless and backed into a corner." Her voice was drowning in a mix of anger and misery.

Zane stilled. "Who's backed you into a corner, Monroe?"

"It doesn't matter." Her voice sounded flat and

resigned. "I have no choice. But I wanted to tell you that I am sorry."

"Let me help you." *Shit, had he really said that?*

"You can't," she whispered harshly. "I wish things were different." She laughed, but it sounded forced. "Anyway, you'll forget me soon enough."

Right then and there, Zane felt like he'd never forget that kiss. It was damn well etched into his soul. What was it about this woman that grabbed him by the throat? Lust? Was it as simple as that?

He tried to tell himself that he didn't know her, and she didn't matter, but it didn't seem to lessen his desire. Or the insane need to help her.

"Monroe, tell me what's going on."

"I can't, or they'll kill him."

This man who wasn't her lover, but who she clearly cared about.

Zane knew he needed to walk away. He'd double up on security, find out from Vander who she was, and then hand this over to the cops.

"Who?" he demanded.

She was silent for a long time. "Look, I just wanted to say sorry. You don't deserve any of this... So, I'm sorry, okay?"

His hand curled on the railing. He wished she was here with him, so he could see her face. So he could convince her to trust him, to let him help her.

At that moment, he realized the thumping song from the dance floor was also coming through the phone line.

He stilled. "Monroe, where are you?"

"It doesn't matter. I have to go."

Across the line, he heard a loud female voice, then laughter.

He scanned the floor below.

"Goodbye, Zane."

"Monroe—"

The line went dead. He set the phone in his pocket, his gaze on the dance floor.

He scanned it, searching.

She was here.

8

DREAM OF ME

Monroe

"**W**oo!" Sabrina clinked her lemon drop martini against mine.

"Cheers." I managed a smile for my veil-wearing, slightly tipsy friend.

Mayfair was full of people. Our group of eight women were all laughing, drinking, and having fun. Well, except for me.

Sabrina was flushed and happy. I was glad she'd found Andrew. They were both cute as hell, and good for each other. Andrew worshipped the ground Sabrina walked on—quirks and all—just as she was.

I sipped my martini. I was wearing a fire-engine-red dress that hugged my body. Sabrina had demanded I wear it. It hugged my body like a possessive lover and had an off-the-shoulder neckline.

I really wasn't in the mood to party.

I'd just apologized to Zane—but I didn't feel any

better. And Mag was still out there in the hands of bad people.

My life sucked.

"Monroe, you need to relax." One of my locksmiths, Kat, appeared. The middle-aged woman was holding a bottle of beer. "This is a party. How often do you get to let your hair down?"

"Ah, never." I had a business to run and a brother to keep out of trouble.

Kat tapped her bottle to my glass. "Live a little."

I managed a smile. God, I wanted to share that Maguire was in danger, that I had to break every single personal value I held, and there was a guy who had me tied up in knots. I blew out a breath, feeling so damn alone, even in the middle of a crowd.

The music changed to one of Sabrina's favorites.

"Let's dance." Sabrina threw her arms in the air, spilling some of her martini.

I was definitely going to have to pour her into a cab at the end of the night.

Reluctantly, I let myself be dragged onto the dance floor. Sabrina was jumping around and laughing.

The dance floor was mostly in shadow, with lights strobing across the floor every now and then. I let the music wash over me. For a second, I was going to pretend my life wasn't a giant mess. For a second, I was going to pretend I was a normal, single woman having a fun time out. Some guys pressed closer, dancing with Sabrina's other friends.

"I'm taken." Sabrina flashed her engagement ring and a wide smile.

Another dancing trio pushed between me and my group.

I edged around, moving to the music, and swinging my hips. I felt the music throb through my blood.

Then a hard body pressed up behind me, and I stiffened.

A strong arm slid around my waist, warm breath on my ear.

"Having fun?"

My stomach clenched.

Zane pulled me back against him, moving in time with me to the music.

Oh, God. Oh, God. He felt so good. Smelled so good.

I was surrounded by him, and for a second, I felt protected.

"You look too good in this dress." His hand slid down the side of my thigh. "I hate any other man looking at you right now."

I closed my eyes and moved my hips, my ass rubbing against him.

"You shouldn't be anywhere near me," I murmured.

"I know."

"What are you doing here?"

"I was enjoying a drink with my friends. Then I spotted the woman who's been driving me crazy. What are you doing here?"

For a second, I couldn't respond. His palm spread out across my belly, his fingers splayed. They felt hot, burning through the fabric of my dress.

"I'm here with my friend. The cute blonde with the curly hair."

"The bride-to-be? She looks like a doll."

"Yes, but don't tell her the doll bit. She hates being cute."

"You aren't cute. You're long, sexy." He tugged on my hair. "And finally, I get to see your real hair. Black suits you better."

I felt the brush of his mouth on the side of my neck. I shuddered, and sensation rolled through me. "*Zane.*"

"I love the way you say my name, Monroe."

The dance floor, the club, the other dancers were just a blur. There was only Zane and me.

I'd never wanted anyone or anything quite as much as I wanted him right now.

The song changed, the beat picking up. The crowd started jumping and Zane spun me, his mouth crashing down on mine.

God. *God.*

I slid my arms around his neck, and we were plastered together.

The kiss turned wild. Voracious, both of us demanding more. The luscious taste of him filled me.

With a moan, I pressed into him, my fingers sinking into his thick hair. His hands slid around and covered my ass, squeezed.

Desire and need were a potent rush between my thighs. My panties were damp in a flash.

The kiss stole my breath, my senses, everything. My need was hot and vicious. I sucked on his tongue, and he growled into my mouth.

He nipped my bottom lip, then dove into the kiss again.

I couldn't get enough. He pulled me closer, and I felt the hard erection against my belly.

"Come home with me," he murmured.

I barely heard him over the music.

"Let me have you, Monroe."

Pulling my lips from his physically hurt. "I can't."

Maguire. My brother's name was like a dash of cold water. Hard, harsh reality rolled right back in.

Zane's hands tightened on me. "You want to."

I met his gaze. It was burning, and my belly contracted.

It was so hard to pull away from him.

"We don't always get what we want, Zane."

He looked like he wanted to argue. "At least promise you'll call me when you get home. Let me know you made it safely."

I cupped his jaw for a second. Why did he have to be sexy and nice? Then I whirled away, plunging into the dancers, before I gave in and threw myself at him.

Tears threatened.

I needed to find Sabrina and get away from here.

* * *

Zane

Zane stalked into his penthouse.

The lights of New York glinted through the windows. The taste of Monroe was still in his mouth.

She was keeping secrets, just another person who

wanted something from him, and he still couldn't fight this brutal need for her.

He shed his jacket and threw it over the couch, then kicked off his shoes. His skin was hot, and his fingers still tingled from touching her gorgeous body. He unbuttoned his shirt and yanked his belt off.

He was obsessed.

He held his phone like a jewel. Like it was the damn necklace he'd bought for his mom.

The phone rang and he quickly thumbed the button. "Monroe."

Silence. "I made it home." Her voice was breathy.

"Me too. Your friend?"

"I handed her, giggling and tipsy, over to her fiancé." Amusement and love filled her voice.

"Now you're home. Look out the window, that's what I'm doing." He liked the idea of both of them looking at the city.

She snorted. "I don't have your million-dollar view, Roth."

He smiled. "You could be here."

She made a sound. A hitch in her voice. "You'll hate me soon."

He doubted that. "Let me help you."

"Someone's life depends on me." She sighed. "And I'm realizing that you can't escape the past, no matter how much you try. Blood runs true."

Zane frowned and sank onto his couch. He wanted to hear her voice breathless again, not tinged with resignation and pain.

"Are you still wearing that sexy, red dress?"

That startled a laugh out of her. "Yes." A rustle. "And now I'm not."

Zane's blood fired. *Fuck.* "I wish I was there to see you. What do you have on underneath?"

"A tiny, black thong."

He could picture her so clearly. His cock throbbed, painful and hard. He'd pay anything to be with her.

He really wanted to touch her.

"Is that little thong wet?" His voice was a growl.

She gasped. "Yes. Is your cock hard?"

"From the first moment I heard your voice tonight."

Her heavy breathing came across the line. "No one's ever wanted me like you do."

He wished she'd come home with him. Wished she'd let him have her, help her. "Take that thong off, Monroe, and lie on your bed."

That earned him a sexy gasp. "Ok-ay."

She'd done it. Hot blood surged into his cock and it pressed against his zipper.

He pictured her naked on her sheets. "Spread those long, sexy legs for me, baby." A rustle. "Describe your pretty pussy. I finally know that you've got dark hair."

"Yes," she breathed. "I'm dark down there, too, but there isn't much of it. Just a thin strip."

Shit. "Touch it."

Her long moan came across the line.

Fuck. Zane yanked his zipper down and pulled his rock-hard, throbbing cock out. "Damn, baby. I wish you were here, and I wish I had my mouth on you."

She moaned. "Are you hard?"

"As a rock. I'm stroking myself."

She moaned again.

Shit, this dirty phone sex was hotter than his last few sexual encounters. Monroe was turning him inside out.

"Spread those sexy legs, gorgeous. I want you to slide your fingers deep inside your sweet pussy."

Her husky gasp drove him crazy. He gripped his cock hard and pumped.

Her next moan was low and throaty.

"How tight are you?" he growled.

"Tight," she said breathlessly. "But I still feel empty."

"You want my cock?"

She moaned his name. "*Zane.*"

He stroked his cock harder. "Answer me."

"Yes." Another moan. "Are you...jacking off?"

"Hell, yeah. Fisting my cock and imagining how it would feel to thrust inside that sweet pussy you're touching." A groan ripped from his throat.

Monroe moaned again. He could tell she was getting close. He imagined her slim fingers inside her, her body writhing.

"Yes, Monroe. Keep stroking. Say my name when you come."

"I'm...close. Zane."

"God, I love hearing my name on your lips." He stroked himself harder. He felt his own release roaring closer. "Come, Monroe. Come now, baby."

She cried out, then screamed his name.

It was too easy to picture her, her arched body shaking with pleasure, her hand between her thighs.

Zane groaned. Pleasure was like a sharp spike down

his spine. With another hard stroke, he came. "Fuck...Monroe."

Ropes of come spurted from him. He groaned, spilling over his gut.

Then he could just hear Monroe's breathing.

"Did you come?" she asked.

"Yeah. Made a mess."

She made a needy sound. Like she wished she could see it. "I've never had phone sex before."

"The first time for me, too." He'd done a little sexy talk, sure, but never the full deal. "I especially like the part where you screamed my name."

"I liked that bit, too." Her voice was warm and amused.

"I'd like to hear it in person next time," he said.

"Zane—"

He told himself to have patience.

"Sleep now, Monroe. Dream of me."

9
_____

MY WAY IN

Monroe

I woke, stretched, then sat bolt upright in my bed. Sunlight hit my eyes and I cursed.

Oh, jeez. I'd had dirty, filthy phone sex with Zane Roth.

I flopped back and pulled a pillow over my face.

My body tingled, and I felt great. I'd had the best sleep I'd had in days.

The sounds of Zane's groans, knowing that he was stroking that beautiful cock and thinking of me...

This was lust. Just lust. *Right?*

Zane Roth was not for me. If he knew everything about me, my father, and what I was going to do, he'd run as fast as his designer shoes could take him.

I groaned.

A part of me really wished things were different. That we lived in a world where we fit together.

My cell phone rang on my bedside table and I stiffened. It could be Mag's captors.

I grabbed it and saw it was Sabrina.

"Hey," I said.

"Oh my God, I'm dying," Sabrina groaned.

I grinned. "I tried to stop you from having those last few cocktails."

Another moan. "Well, thanks for getting me home."

"Always, Sabrina."

"Did you have fun?"

"Sure. A girls' night out is always fun."

"And so is kissing the brains out of a hunk on the dance floor?"

"What?" I squeaked.

"Spill, Monroe O'Connor."

"I...don't know what you're talking about."

"Jennifer saw you."

Dammit. "I plead the fifth."

"Oh my God, you kissed a hot stranger on the dance floor! You go, girl."

I climbed out of bed. "I'm heading down to the shop shortly." It was Sunday and the shop was closed today. "I need to get a few hours of office work done."

"Okay, keep your hot-guy secrets."

Crap, if Sabrina ever discovered the truth, she'd lose her mind.

"Hey, how's Mag?" Sabrina asked.

My gut twisted. I hated lying to my friend. "Oh, you know, being Mag."

"He needs to grow up," Sabrina said dryly.

No, he needed to survive. "I know. Love you."

"Love you, Monroe. I *will* get the details of your dance-floor kiss out of you one day." Sabrina sounded determined.

She was cute, but she could be tenacious.

"You're going to find the perfect guy one day," Sabrina continued. "Who stands up to you, supports you, and doesn't let you walk all over him, but most of all, loves you, no matter what."

A wave of sadness hit me. I felt like a hand closed around my throat. Unfortunately, I'd met a man who matched the first part of that description, but would never be the last bit. There was no happy ending for the daughter of a con artist thief and a billionaire.

I showered, changed, and made a piece of toast that I slathered with jelly. I spied a leftover cupcake and shrugged. *Why the hell not?* I bit into it and went downstairs.

Time to get back to work on the Riv3000.

I was dragging my feet. I knew I couldn't let my feelings for Zane interfere with what I had to do.

Mag was depending on me. The deadline was looming.

As I munched on the cupcake, I saw the newspaper was sitting on the front step of the shop, and I went out to get it. My dad had always read the newspaper, and had said he liked the feel of it in his hands. Looking back, he was probably using it to scout out jobs.

When I lifted the paper, I saw the manilla folder under it and my heart skipped a beat. I recognized Mac's scratchy writing. The man did everything old school, and didn't believe in email.

I flicked open the folder and saw Monica Gorman's life spread out in detail. I read it and then I read it again.

Back inside, the store was quiet and hushed. I liked it when it was closed and no one was in there. I looked around at the gleaming shelves and cabinets.

Mine.

All mine.

When I'd first opened it, I'd been so proud. When I'd first turned a profit and saw a good, legitimate way to make a living, it had made me so happy.

It hurt that I had to put it at risk and commit a crime. My hand clenched on the file.

When I reached my office, I flicked the light on. The skeleton of the safe sat there, taunting me. I put on the kettle I kept in the corner to make some tea. If I drank coffee all day, I'd get jittery.

Idly, I flicked through the newspaper while I waited for the water to boil. A familiar face caught my eye.

My heart did a jig. *Zane*.

He looked smiling and handsome in a tuxedo. Heat licked my belly. The man looked good enough to eat. The next picture had my happy feelings curdling.

A stylish blonde in a sleek dress was under his arm.

I scanned the text. Socialite Ariana Waldman. Daughter of some rich family. The article speculated about when the couple would get engaged.

Carefully, I folded the paper, then tossed it in the trash.

Ariana was exactly the kind of woman Zane should be with. Volatile emotions rocketed around inside me. *So stupid.*

Taking a breath, I yanked the paper back out of the trash can and looked at it again.

He was going to be at a fancy, charity ball tonight. Ariana Waldman was attending, as well. Jeez, how many parties and balls did he go to every week?

And how many women did he kiss and seduce every week?

You aren't special, Monroe. Yes, I was a total idiot. I stabbed my pen through Ariana's beautiful face.

I lifted my chin, then sat down at my desk. I had a job to do.

Swiveling back to the safe, I pressed a palm to it. It would be very different cracking this modern safe than Mr. Goldstein's Rosengrens. I needed a whole different set of tools.

I picked up my autodialer. Rollo had helped me create the device. I hooked it up to my Riv3000 replica. It needed a little more tweaking to be matched to the safe. Then it would run through combinations to find Zane's code.

Tapping my fingers on my desk, I watched the autodialer whiz through numbers. I'd also need to bypass the biometric fingerprint lock as well. And I also needed a way into Zane's penthouse.

For once, I didn't feel any pleasure in cracking a safe.

The autodialer stopped and the safe clicked open. *Bingo.* I checked everything again. Then again.

On the next try, I timed the autodialer. I'd need to shave a few seconds off the time.

The sound of Zane's voice, the feel of his body, the

taste of his lips clouded my head. I cursed. Maguire was the only man I should be thinking about.

My phone rang and I saw that it was a private number.

"Hello?" I asked warily.

"Sleep well?" Zane drawled, his voice like warm chocolate.

Anger, jealousy, and hurt all coalesced inside me. "Fine."

My sharp tone made him pause. "What's wrong?"

"Nothing. Things just were made extra clear to me this morning." I sighed, feeling tired. So damn tired. "Things I already knew, but was being stupid about."

"Talk to me, Monroe."

The way he said my name... I steeled myself. "I was just reading about your impending engagement."

Silence.

I felt my heart shrivel. "I hope you'll be happy, and you should quit kissing strange women on dance floors."

"My what?" He sounded angry.

I lifted my chin. It was just because he had been called out. "Your engagement. To Ariana Waldman."

"Monroe, the press writes shit about me daily. I stood next to Ariana at a party recently. I've spoken to her maybe a dozen times."

I closed my eyes. I wanted to believe him.

This is the last job, Monny. I promise. You, Mag, and me, we'll live the high life after this one. No more jobs for your da. We're going to be a real family, baby girl.

I'd been raised by the best liar in the world. I'd

learned not to listen to halfhearted promises that I was so desperate to hear.

"Monroe?"

"Goodbye, Zane."

He cursed. "Monroe, don't—"

I ended the call.

Shakily, I grabbed my ball cap and pulled it on, then grabbed my keys, phone, and the file on Monica Gorman. I was out the door in seconds.

I had to focus on the job.

I'd been stalling.

I had to steal the necklace.

Zane wouldn't be at home this evening. He'd be busy at the ball, and I'd be busy cracking his safe and stealing the Phillips-Morley necklace.

Tonight.

It had to be tonight.

I rode my bike to Billionaire's Row, and continued past his building.

Right on time, a brunette in designer jeans, blue shirt, and beige blazer stepped outside. She wheeled a small suitcase behind her with a briefcase balanced on top, and was talking on the phone.

In an alley, I stashed my bike and chained it up. I rounded the corner, walking briskly.

The woman approached.

According to Mac, who'd no doubt interrogated anyone who knew the woman, Monica Gorman kept a clockwork schedule. The lawyer worked every day of the week, including a few hours on Sunday. After she worked today, she'd then meet her friends-with-benefits lover for a movie or a show, followed by dinner and an overnight stay at his place.

"Yes, I need all those case files before the trial. Yes, do it today, Lainie." A pause. "Yes, I know it's Sunday. The law never sleeps, rests, or goes out for Sunday brunch."

I shifted a little closer, eyeing the woman's handbag slung over her shoulder.

Monica clipped me, her handbag flying off and hitting the sidewalk. Items spilled everywhere.

"God. Sorry." The brunette spun, and crouched down to pick up her things.

"It's fine." I squatted as well, helping gather the items. "You need to watch where you're going."

The woman made an annoyed noise. "Right. I apologize."

I handed her a notebook, a tube of lipstick, and a pack of tissues.

"Thanks." The woman snatched them, shoved them in her bag, and went right back to talking on the phone. "Sorry, I'm here—"

She disappeared down the street.

Monica Gorman lived three floors below Zane's penthouse.

I slid my hand into my pocket, and fingered the key card that I'd just pickpocketed.

I now had Monica's key, and my way in.

Monroe

I sat in the coffee shop across the street, watching Zane's building. Evening had fallen, and his building looked busy. Lots of rich people heading in and out.

Biting my lip, I made myself think of Maguire. I'd gotten another picture of him, looking tired and scared, but thankfully, unhurt.

At least for now. The clock was ticking and I was running out of time.

"Hang in there, little brother," I whispered.

Across the street, I saw a couple exit the building. The man had his arm around the woman, holding her securely. The woman beamed up at him.

My belly hurt with an ache I couldn't control. I'd never had a relationship like that. What would it be like to know that someone had your back? That they were there for you, to grab you if you fell?

Then I saw a limo—sleek and black—slide up and stop in front of the building.

A second later, Zane strode out of the doors, heading for the car.

My chest locked. God, he looked good. He was in a tuxedo, and he looked too handsome to be real. Way out of my league.

I watched him slip into the limo. The car pulled away, and I stared after it until I couldn't see the taillights anymore.

Game time.

I paid for my coffee, then strode out across the street.

I was dressed in an expensive, black, ankle-length coat, and high heels.

I put some swagger in my step. My father had taught me that the best cons worked because you believed that you were the character you were playing. That you believed that you belonged.

Pulse rabbiting, I sailed through the lobby and into the elevator. I held my stolen keycard up to the reader.

Beep.

The doors closed and the elevator zoomed upward. I got out and glanced up.

Only three floors to where I needed to be.

I entered Monica's apartment. It was done in lots of shades of white, and like Zane's, had a killer view of Central Park.

I slipped off my heels and pulled the coat off. Underneath, I wore tight, black leggings and a snug black shirt. I was also wearing my toolbelt. I draped my coat over a chair and set my heels down beside it. Next, I pulled out my rubber-soled climbing socks from my bag.

In Monica's dining room, I looked at the vent in the ceiling that was part of the central-air system. It was right above the shiny, dining room table.

I climbed up, and pulled a tool off my belt.

With a quick whirr, I pulled the screws out and yanked the vent grate off.

Then I gripped the edge and pulled myself up.

With a grunt, I settled in the vent. It wasn't exactly spacious, but I fit. I started crawling.

I'd memorized the schematics for the building's ventilation system. Another thing I owed Rollo cupcakes for this time.

I crawled along for several feet, and came to a vertical vent. I pressed my feet to the walls and started climbing. Soon, my muscles burned, and I knew I'd feel it tomorrow.

Argh. I pulled myself up into a horizontal vent and stopped to catch my breath. Then I kept crawling.

After twenty minutes of squeezing my ass through tight spots and climbing, I stopped.

If my calculations were correct...

I peered down through the grate.

And saw the expanse of Zane's marble kitchen island.

I sucked in a breath and pulled out my tool again.

Once the grate was off, I gripped the edge and rolled down like a gymnast.

My feet touched marble, and I dropped into a crouch on the middle of his island.

Time to steal a necklace from the man I found endlessly fascinating. I felt a punch of sorrow, but squelched it. Mag's life was on the line.

I made my way quickly through the amazing penthouse, pausing once to look out the windows at the park again. Memories of that kiss rocked me.

I averted my gaze and forced myself to focus on the task.

Zane had left a few lights on, and I moved quickly down the hall.

He was no doubt pressed up against some beautiful socialite. Sexy billionaires could have anyone they wanted. I had to stop thinking about him.

I headed for his office, but stopped and eyed the door at the end of the hall.

I shouldn't get distracted.

Looking down, I glanced at the low glow of my watch. I had a little time. He'd be at the ball for hours.

I walked quickly and silently, then stepped into the master bedroom.

Sucking in a breath, I succeeded in pulling in the scent of Zane. His cologne, but also *him*—sexy male.

The carpet was soft under my feet as I walked farther into the room. The bed was draped in moonlight.

I could easily picture two bodies entwined on the covers—me and Zane.

Muttering a curse, I stepped into his master closet. The man sure had a lot of clothes. I fingered his suits, shirts. One shirt was tossed over a chair, and I lifted and sniffed.

His scent was strong and my body responded, a flash of heat between my legs. I pressed my thighs together.

He affected me so easily. Why him? I dropped the shirt. God, I was standing here, sniffing his shirt like an idiot.

That said, he'd affect any woman over the age of five.

But I also thought of his smile, the intense look in his eyes, the way he moved that lean, powerful body.

His love for his mom and his loyalty to his friends.

The way he'd offered to help me.

I spotted some jewelry drawers. They had locks that were ridiculously easy to pop.

Rolex. Patek Philippe. Rolex. Holy cow, a Lange & Söhne Grand Complication. This watch was worth over two million dollars. Did he casually walk around with that on his wrist?

Shaking my head, I fingered the watches, then some cufflinks.

Who needed this many watches and cufflinks?

Before I could stop myself, I slipped out a Rolex. It was a simple Submariner. I stroked the face, knowing he'd worn it.

With a sigh, I set it back on the velvet, then closed the drawer and headed out.

Now, I needed to get my job done and get gone.

I entered the office, and saw the desk lamp was on.

I eyed the Riv3000. *Hello, there.*

I pulled a cell phone-like device out of my pouch. Another little tool that Rollo had helped me with. I moved to the phone on the desk and turned on the small, hand-held scanner. I waved the light across the phone.

Beep.

Got it. I looked at the scanner screen and saw a perfect, digital replica of Zane's fingerprint.

I sank to my knees in front of the safe and pulled out my tools.

Then I got to work.

My father had taught me to take my time. Each safe had its own personality, its own quirks.

It paid to get to know them, then use the knowledge against them.

I attached the autodialer and set it working. Then I held the scanner fingerprint to the biometric lock.

Nothing happened.

Come on. I shifted it a little.

The biometric lock beeped.

I smiled and watched the autodialer as the numbers clicked by. I smoothed my palm over the metal.

"Let me in, little lady."

The numbers stopped. *Click*.

My pulse spiked. I'd done it. I'd just cracked the Riv3000. I opened the safe door.

And saw the necklace box inside.

I lifted my hand...

And heard a sound echo through the penthouse.

I rose, my heart hammering in my chest. I stepped into the hall and cocked my head.

"I'm fine, I just got home." Zane's deep voice. "I'm not in the mood for a fucking party, Liam."

Fuck. Zane was home.

"No, but I see I have an email from Vander." A pause. "Maybe I am stalling from reading it."

I had no time. I had to go.

His footsteps got closer and I glanced back into the office. *Shit*.

Think, Monroe, think.

Then I looked up.

Zane was at the end of the hall, and his gaze met mine.

Shit.

I turned and ran in the opposite direction.

10

EXPLOSIONS

Zane

Monroe.

She was dressed all in black, staring at him with wide eyes.

Then, she ran.

Zane's heart thundered, and he sprinted down the hall after her. He cast a quick glance in his office and saw the open safe.

Hell, no. She wasn't getting away from him.

She darted through a door, and Zane chased her.

"You can't run, Monroe."

"I sure as hell can," she called back.

He almost slipped on the wood floor and cursed his dress shoes. He was still in his tuxedo.

He caught the doorjamb and pushed off.

She darted across the living room on those long legs of hers and circled the coffee table, aiming for the elevator.

Zane leaped over the couch and darted left to cut her off.

She angled away and ran into the hall leading to the guest rooms. He saw her rush into a bedroom and slam the door.

He shoved his hands against the wood, just as he heard the snick of the lock.

"Monroe!" He shoved the door again and it rattled. "Let me in."

"No!"

"I'm going to catch you." He leaned his head against the wood. "Come out. We'll talk."

There was a long pause. "There's nothing to talk about."

Anger punched through him. This woman twisted him up, made him angry, happy, frustrated, turned on.

"Come out, baby. Time to tell me exactly what is going on."

"It's best if I stay far away from you, Zane. For your sake."

He loved the way she said his name. "Not going to happen." He waited. "Monroe?"

There was no answer.

He frowned. There was nowhere for her to go.

"Monroe?"

His chest locked. The only way out of that guestroom was out the window.

His gut cramped. She wouldn't. They were seventy-two stories up.

Fuck.

He sprinted back to the living room and up the stairs.

As he reached the top, he was just in time to see her sprinting along the terrace.

Fucking hell. He was going to strangle her for risking herself like that.

He raced toward her. She saw him, sprinted farther along, and then darted past his outdoor kitchen. Shit, she was quick.

By the time he'd circled the couch, she was sprinting back down the stairs.

"Monroe, I'm not going to stop until I catch you."

She sprinted down the hall and into his bedroom.

Zane followed, and spied a flash of movement. She was going into his bathroom.

The door was closing, but he shoved his foot in the way. She shoved hard and he heard her grunt.

"Monroe," he growled.

"Zane, just walk out of here."

"Not today." He shoved back and the door opened a few inches.

"I told you things are complicated." She shoved the door back toward him.

He gritted his teeth. Damn, she was strong. "So explain it to me."

"You should run. Far and fast. I'm no good for you."

"Because you're a thief." He shoved the door again.

"I am not!" she paused. "Or at least I don't want to be." She shoved back.

"Monroe, come out," he growled.

"I can't get arrested. I... Someone's depending on me. I can't let them down."

Zane scowled. "I'm not going to call the police."

"Then you're an idiot."

"*Monroe.*" God, he was losing his temper. "If you come out here, I'm more likely to kiss the hell out of you than hand you over to the cops."

He heard her suck in a breath.

"I want to do more than kiss you. I want to explore that long, sexy body of yours. Kiss you, stroke you." Desire was a tight coil in his gut. "I want to know what you taste like between your legs. See that little strip of hair you teased me with. I want to watch your face when I sink my cock inside you."

"Zane." A helpless, husky whisper.

"I want to feel you on my cock when you scream my name."

"Stop it," she whispered.

"I want to help you with whatever trouble you're in."

Silence again.

"No one ever helps me."

Zane barely heard her whisper. "Just reach out. I'm right here."

"I don't know how."

He tried to imagine what she'd lived through before, with no one to help her. Even when it had just been him and his mom, they'd leaned on each other. Then he'd had Mav and Liam.

Zane snaked his arm through the gap in the door, hoping she wouldn't slam it on his arm.

His fingers wrapped around her slender wrist, and he felt her tremble.

Slowly, he pulled on her and opened the door.

Stormy, gray eyes met his. She looked ridiculously

good all in black, like her silky hair, that was currently pulled back in a long ponytail.

He tugged her into the bedroom and pushed her against the wall, pinning her with his body.

"Hey," he said.

"Hi," she whispered back.

"You look extremely sexy for a cat burglar."

She rolled her eyes. "How many cat burglars do you know?"

"One." He kissed her.

She made a hungry sound, then her hands fisted in his hair.

"Tell me your full name." He knew he had an email from Vander waiting for him, which no doubt held her name and her entire history, but Zane really wanted to hear it from her.

"No." She pressed her lips to his.

The kiss exploded.

Desire raced through Zane like a firestorm.

With a groan, he pressed closer, and her tongue tangled with his. He cupped her ass and she jumped up, her long legs wrapping around his waist.

Thank God.

He pinned her to the wall again and she rubbed her body against him, the juncture of her thighs to his throbbing cock.

"Oh, *God*." The back of her head hit the wall.

"Name," he demanded.

She just moaned.

He groaned. "Right there." He rubbed against her and she let out a husky cry. "You like my cock right there, don't you, Monroe?"

"Yes, damn you."

He kept rubbing his cock right between her thighs, only the thin layers of clothes between them. He moved one hand to cup her high, firm breast.

She made the sexiest sound he'd ever heard, and he felt her tense.

Then she exploded for him.

With savage satisfaction, he watched the orgasm take her. He held her body as she shook through her pleasure.

"You have a quick trigger, baby." He was pleased that he could bring her to pleasure so fast.

She blinked and her cheeks flushed. "*God.*" She shoved him backward.

She'd surprised him, and he almost fell. Cursing, he caught his balance, just in time to see her run out the door.

"Dammit, Monroe. Stop!"

He chased her down the hall. Ahead, he saw her stumble to a stop near his office. She turned, her face turning white as a sheet.

He frowned.

Then she charged back at him. She slammed into him, shoving him hard.

Zane stumbled into a guest room doorway, just as the world exploded in smoke, heat, and flames.

Monroe

I hit the floor hard, my ears ringing.

Shit. Shit. Shit.

I'd seen the bomb sitting right on Zane's big desk, and just reacted.

My only thought had been to get Zane out of the way. I pushed myself up, trying to clear my head.

Had I gotten him out of the blast zone? My heart was in my throat as I looked up.

I saw his legs. He was lying flat on his back, dust covering his tuxedo pants. He wasn't moving.

I couldn't breathe. *Be okay. Please be okay.*

I crawled over to him. His eyes were closed, and I pressed a palm to his chest.

When I felt the steady rise and fall, the air rushed out of me. I touched his neck with shaking fingers and found his pulse, strong and steady.

"Thank God." Relief made me feel dizzy. I moved up and touched my lips to his.

Then I lifted my head and spotted figures moving through the smoke. The entire wall of his office had been blown apart, and ceiling panels had collapsed.

Heart racing, I stayed still, crouched over Zane.

Figures were in the office. Near the safe.

The safe I'd left open.

Oh, shit.

While the intruders were busy, I grabbed Zane under his arms and heaved.

Ugh, he was heavy. I bent my legs and pulled. Inch

by inch, I dragged him toward the bed, then shoved him under it.

Footsteps.

I leaped over the bed and crouched.

I waited, my heart hammering like a drum. *Who the hell were these assholes?*

Carefully, I peered over the bed, but couldn't see anyone. I reached under the bed and touched Zane again, then I crept toward the doorway. Through the ruined wall into the office, I heard voices.

"Safe was open."

"Just get the necklace. We only have a few minutes until security and the authorities arrive."

Dammit. I bit my lip. One, these assholes had the necklace. Two, I couldn't be in here when the police arrived.

I watched one of the three men pull out the necklace box. The man opened it.

Through the murk, I couldn't see the necklace clearly, but I saw something glitter in the man's hands.

"Why did we still use the bomb?" a man asked. "We didn't need to blow the safe."

"Covers our tracks." A low laugh. "And I like making a mess."

"Let's go," another man snapped.

They all had accents. French, maybe, or Italian. Who were they? I'd been blackmailed into this theft, but now there were other players in the game.

"Someone must be here," one man said.

"Just get the damn thing and move."

"I could do a sweep and check."

"No time."

The men strode away, taking the necklace with them.

My chin dropped to my chest.

That necklace was the only way to save Mag, and now it was gone.

Dammit to hell.

I raced back to Zane and pulled him out from under the bed. I grunted from the strain, but got him out.

He was still unconscious.

I stroked his cheek and then grabbed a pillow off the bed and slid it under his head.

"I have to go. Help's coming."

I rose, and darted out of the room and into the office. I spied my autodialer under some rubble, grabbed it, and slipped it back on my belt.

For a beat, I stared at the empty safe, then back at the room where Zane was.

Then I ran into the living area.

I moved toward the emergency stairwell doorway, and shoved it open.

Then I heard the echo of voices below.

"We need those extinguishers. Move, people."

Firefighters.

I raced back inside, then climbed back onto the island and leaped into the vent. I set the grate back in place, but there was no time to screw it in.

It was a bit smoky, but I crawled through.

It felt like it took forever before I was climbing back into Monica's apartment. I replaced the grate, thinking of Zane the entire time.

Was he okay? They would've found him by now.

I pulled on my coat and slid my heels back on. I fixed my hair and headed to the door. I glanced at the hall mirror and frowned at the sight of soot all over my face. *Dammit.*

I ducked into the guest bathroom and took a second to clean up. Then I slipped out of the apartment, down the corridor, and into the stairwell.

There were loads of people evacuating, and I listened to the panic and speculation echoing around me.

Finally, I reached the ground floor, and joined the crowds on the sidewalk.

I knew that I should get the hell out of here. There was already a fire engine out front, and, as I watched, several police cars screeched to a halt. I stiffened as I saw an ambulance pull in, sirens blaring.

Where was Zane?

I tucked myself into a large knot of people and watched, gnawing on my bottom lip. What if he'd hit his head really badly? What if he was hurt and I hadn't realized?

Now, a slew of reporters had arrived, with tons of cameras, jostling at the barriers. They were shouting questions at the police.

A sleek, red sports car pulled up and Maverick Rivera climbed out. His face looked like stone.

A bit later, a limousine also pulled up, and Liam Kensington got out, buttoning his jacket.

Both billionaires ignored the reporters and headed through the front door of Zane's building.

A moment later they reappeared, followed by Zane, with a paramedic by his side.

His face was incandescent with rage.

I gasped. My pleasure at seeing him evaporated.

Another man stalked out of the crowd and I felt a lick of fear. He was a few inches over six feet, with a muscular body, and he radiated badass vibes that set the hairs on the back of my neck rising. His suit didn't do much to tone down the sense that he was dangerous. The kind of person you didn't want to piss off. He greeted the men, then scanned the crowd.

I forced myself not to duck.

Zane gestured, then the four men disappeared back into the lobby.

Shit, did he think I was responsible for the bomb? I sagged. He hadn't seen the intruders.

I pressed a hand to my temple, feeling sick.

Then I turned and walked through the crowd. The bystanders were all filled with curiosity and excitement. I felt like I was about to puke.

It was better this way. He wouldn't want anything to do with me.

This was safer for him.

Besides, I needed to focus on how the hell I could save my brother.

I had no necklace. No idea who'd taken it.

As I walked down the street, I felt the most alone I ever had in my life.

I looked back up at the spear of 111 West 57th Street.

Goodbye, Zane.

11

HER NAME IS MONROE O'CONNOR

Zane

Zane ground his teeth together. Rage clung around his throat like barbed wire.

Monroe had blown up his damn penthouse.

She'd almost killed him, and herself.

And damned if it wasn't the last thing that pissed him off the most.

What if she was hurt?

Anger burst in his chest. He had to stop thinking about her.

A paramedic hovered over him. "Mr. Roth—"

"I'm fine." His voice echoed in the lobby.

"You took a hard hit to the head, Mr. Roth," the paramedic continued. "You might have a concussion—"

"I've had a concussion before, and I'm fine."

"You sure?" Mav asked.

"Let him check you over," Liam suggested.

"There's no blood and nothing's broken." Zane met Vander Norcross' dark gaze. "What are you doing here?"

"I was in New York for business, and I figured I'd check in with you." His dark-blue eyes scanned Zane. "Looks like my instincts were right."

Vander had some damn spooky instincts. He'd led a covert Ghost Ops team—a military team made up of the best of the best from special forces units across all branches of the military. The guy was good.

"What the fuck happened?" Mav asked.

"I left the charity ball early...and I found Monroe in my apartment."

Liam looked at the ceiling.

"She'd cracked your safe, by the way," Zane told Maverick.

Mav cursed. "Impossible."

"She was after the necklace I bought for my mom."

"Fuck," Mav snapped.

Vander was watching him—his face an impassive mask. "What happened next?"

"She tried to kill me."

"Step by step, Zane."

Zane scraped a hand through his hair. "I caught her. I chased her. Then..."

Shit, he didn't want to share exactly what they'd done against the wall in his room.

Liam rolled his eyes and Mav made an angry sound.

"You catch a thief robbing you of millions Roth, you don't fuck her."

"I didn't. It didn't...go that far." Zane shook his head. "She's in some kind of trouble."

"She had the necklace?" Vander continued.

"No." Zane frowned. "She was running and reached my office, then she jumped on me and everything exploded. When I came to, there were firefighters everywhere."

"Let's check your security footage," Vander said.

"Mr. Roth?" A firefighter stepped forward. "I'm Lieutenant Nathan Bassett. The bomb dogs have been through your penthouse, and it's clear. It appears that there was only one small device detonated in your office. The wall and ceiling in your office aren't stable. I'd suggest you stay elsewhere while it's repaired."

Zane gave the man a tired nod. "Thank you."

"The police also have some questions."

Fuck. "Okay. Can I get some of my things?"

"Of course."

Zane spoke with the police detectives—an older, rumpled one and his younger, clean-cut partner—and made no mention of Monroe. He rolled it over in his head. He should give them her name.

"I came home early from the Food and Wine Gala—"

"The one that supports Prevention of Cruelty to Children?" Detective Brown murmured. "At the Metropolitan Club."

Zane nodded.

"Good charity."

"When I got home, I disturbed some thieves. After that, everything exploded. I don't know what happened."

The shrewd eyes of the older detective stared at him for a beat. "You have security cameras?"

"Yes. Norcross here put the security in. We're going

to see if anything is salvageable. If so, I'll give you a call, Detective Brown."

The detective grunted and handed over a card. "Glad you weren't hurt, Mr. Roth."

"Because he has a hard fucking head," Mav muttered.

The four of them took the elevator up.

When the doors opened, the strong smell of smoke assaulted his nostrils. Black, sooty footprints covered his floor.

Shit. He'd need to call a team in to come tomorrow and clean what they could, and a contractor to shore up the walls and ceiling in his office.

Vander wandered into his kitchen, paused, then looked up.

"What?" Zane asked.

The man pointed at the marble island.

Two perfect, small, narrow footprints marred the surface.

"She likely got in and out through the air vent," Vander said.

Zane eyed the small vent. Hell, she was more resourceful than he'd given her credit for.

They headed down the hall. When he saw the mess that remained of his office, his gut tightened.

Mav cursed and Liam whistled.

"Damn, Roth," Mav said. "You're lucky you weren't killed."

Vander scanned the ruins, hands on his lean hips.

Then he strode back to the living room.

The main security hub was hidden in a built-in cupboard in the wall. Vander opened a small pin pad and tapped in a code. He'd overseen the installation of the entire system.

"Office camera was destroyed, but the one in the hall is fine. Looks like we have office footage up to the explosion." He pulled out a tablet and tapped.

Zane leaned over. Mav and Liam did the same from the other side.

The footage showed Monroe crouched in front of the safe. She was working on it, and a second later, the door opened.

"Fucking hell," Mav said. "I want to know how she did it."

Monroe stood suddenly.

Another camera angle showed Zane arriving home. Then he watched their mad chase through the penthouse.

Liam broke out in a low chuckle, Vander's lips twitched, and Mav growled.

"Shut it. All of you."

There was no camera in his room, so there was a little while of nothing.

"Hello," Vander murmured.

Another camera showed three men entering Zane's apartment from the emergency stairwell.

"Who the fuck are they?" Zane said. "And how did they get in?"

"I'll be finding out the answers to those questions," Vander murmured.

Zane watched them head for his office. One set a device on his desk.

His chest locked. These men had brought the bomb, not Monroe.

The men had a brief conversation, clearly confused by the open safe. Then one waved them out of the room. They hustled into the living room and ducked down behind the couches.

Monroe appeared in the hall.

He watched as she spotted the bomb, turned, and leaped on Zane, knocking him down.

The wall exploded.

"She knocked you out of the way," Vander said.

Zane stared, his heart pounding loudly in his ears.

"You would've been in line with the office when the bomb went off, otherwise," Mav said, dully.

"Look." Vander switched the camera feed.

Zane watched as Monroe scrambled to check him, stroked his face, then kissed him.

Then she dragged him into the guestroom.

She'd protected him.

She'd risked herself to save him.

He watched the thieves go back into the office, get the necklace, then leave. Then he watched Monroe climb back into the vent a second before the firefighters burst in.

His friends were silent.

Zane's hands balled into a fist. "Vander, I want her name and address."

"Check your email." Vander's dark-blue gaze met Zane's. "Her name is Monroe O'Connor."

Zane's heart skipped a beat. *Finally.* "And find these fuckers who blew up my place and stole my necklace."

A scary smile crossed Vander's features. "My pleasure."

Monroe

I staggered into Lady Locksmith the next day in dire need of coffee.

I hadn't slept. I felt sick to my stomach.

I'd been checking online for any news that Zane was okay. He had to think the worst of me now, and that made my heart hurt.

But I had to stop thinking of Zane, because the person who wouldn't be okay was Maguire.

I sagged against the counter. I had to wait for the Russians to contact me. I hoped to hell that I could make a new deal.

My week was almost up. My mouth went dry.

Miserable, I headed to the coffee pot. I was so grateful that it was Sabrina's day off. My friend would take one look at me and know things were terribly wrong.

I poured myself a cup of coffee and drank the first mug standing up.

I forced thoughts of Zane and the necklace out of my head. I needed to schedule jobs for my locksmiths and unpack new stock, and then maybe stress over the mess of my life.

The door jangled. "Morning, Monroe."

The cheery voice made me spin. Chloe Boyd was a teenage girl who helped me out sometimes.

"Hey, Chloe. How's school?" She was in her first year at a local college.

"Awesome." The skinny brunette grinned. "I love college and I aced my test last week."

"Go you."

"College boys are annoying, but cute." Chloe stared at me. "You look terrible, Monroe."

"Thanks." I curtsied.

"You need a better foundation. It'll hide those dark circles."

I forced a smile. If only a new foundation could solve my problems.

"Where's your hunky brother?" Chloe asked, fluttering her eyelashes.

"Oh, he's been away. I have some stock to unpack out back. You got the shop?"

"Sure thing."

"Mondays are usually pretty quiet."

I set to work unpacking boxes. My stress levels were through the roof.

When my cell phone rang, I stiffened. I took a deep breath and grabbed it.

The display read, *unknown caller*.

"Hello?"

"Ms. O'Connor. Have you got the item?" the robot voice asked.

I dragged in another deep breath and dropped to sit on one of the boxes. "There was another team of thieves there."

Silence.

My nerves were alive and itching. "I cracked the safe,

but these guys blew the place up, and took the necklace. You never said anything about other players being involved."

The silence stretched on. Nausea swelled in my stomach.

"So, you don't have the necklace?"

"No. These guys almost *killed* me. You should've warned me."

"A shame. No necklace, no brother."

My hand squeezed on the phone until I heard the plastic creak. "This wasn't my fault. Don't you dare hurt him!"

"You're in no position to negotiate, Ms. O'Connor."

"I'll steal something else—"

"I want the necklace."

I bit back tears of frustration. "It's gone. I have no idea who has it."

"Find out, Ms. O'Connor. Get the necklace, or Maguire dies."

The line went dead.

"Argh." I barely resisted throwing the phone against the wall.

Assholes.

I pinched the bridge of my nose. At least Mag still had some time.

But the enormity of the task hit me. I had no idea where the necklace was, or who had it.

I released a shaky breath. I needed to pull it together and make a plan.

Finally, I headed out to help Chloe. One of my locksmiths called with a problem. Mr. Goldstein arrived with a cheeky smile.

"Mr. Goldstein. I'm glad you came. I'll have Chloe show you some locks."

"Thank you, Monroe." The older man cocked his head. "You look tired and sad."

I sent him a shaky smile. "Can't fool you. I'll be fine." *Maybe.*

But as I walked into my office, I felt alone. So alone.

As always, I had no one to lean on. No mother. An absent father. And an unreliable brother.

I thought of Zane.

No.

Locking down that thought, I got online and checked the news sites. There was lots of speculation over the disturbance at Zane's place. There was also a picture of him walking on the street this morning, and he looked fine.

I'd half-expected the cops to show up. Surely, he would have told them about me. Strangely, there was no mention of the theft of the necklace in the news reports.

The shop emptied out after a small lunchtime rush. Chloe stood at the counter, munching on some sushi.

My belly was tied up in knots that would do a Boy Scout proud. There was no way I could eat. I fixed a display of funky keychains on the counter.

The door jangled.

I heard Chloe gasp. "Oh, my God, you're Zane Roth."

I didn't stop to think. I simply dropped to the floor in a crouch.

No. No. No. He couldn't be here. In my shop.

Panicked, I crawled across the floor behind the counter. Chloe looked at me like I'd gone crazy.

I circled the counter. Not far to my office. I just needed to get to...

I rammed into a pair of suit-clad legs.

Then strong hands pulled me up.

Hazel eyes stared at me. The gold flecks in them looked even brighter today.

"You found me," I said.

"My private investigator tracked you down, Monroe O'Connor."

My heart sank. He knew who I was. Who my father was.

I felt Chloe staring at us. Zane glanced around the shop. "I like your store."

"Zane—"

"I want you to come with me."

"No." I dropped my voice to a whisper. "I didn't take the necklace—"

"I know."

Damn him for smelling so good. I pressed my hands to his chest. "Go away. Far away."

"No."

Ugh. He was so damn stubborn. "I'm a thief," I whisper-yelled.

"Oh? What have you stolen?"

"Fine. I'm an *almost* thief. I'm the daughter of a thief."

"And I'm the son of a deadbeat, who I haven't spoken to in years."

I growled. "Zane—"

"Oh, God. I can't believe Zane Roth is in *here*." Chloe moved closer. "Can I take a selfie with you?"

"No!" I cried.

Chloe blinked.

I pressed a hand to my head. "Sorry, Chloe, I—"

"Monroe's coming with me." Zane shot the teenager a charming smile. "Can you hold down the fort, Chloe?"

The traitorous girl nodded.

I shook my head. "No, I'm not—"

Zane dipped, pressed a shoulder to my torso, then lifted me off my feet.

Next thing I knew, I found myself tossed over his shoulder.

Unbelievable. I gasped. "Put me down, Roth."

"No."

He slapped a hand to my ass and strode out of the shop.

"Put me down right now—"

"I warned you that I'd catch you, Monroe. Now, you're all mine."

12

SMUG, BOSSY BILLIONAIRES

Zane

Zane strode down the street, holding tight to a wriggling Monroe.

He stopped beside his black Bugatti Chiron, bleeped the locks, and dumped her in the passenger seat.

He slid into the driver's seat.

"Where the hell do you get off, Roth?" She twisted in the seat. "You can't just carry a woman out of her place of business and throw her in your—" she glanced around "—very expensive car. How much is this car worth?"

"You probably don't want to know." He pulled out. "I find you aren't a great listener, so I needed to get your attention."

She crossed her arms over her chest. "I'm a brilliant listener. The best."

"We're going somewhere quiet, with no interruptions, and you're going to tell me what the hell is going on."

She shot him a mutinous look and Zane wanted to kiss her.

"Are you okay?" he asked. "After the bomb?" He reached out and touched her hand.

She let out a noisy breath and turned her hand into his. "Yes. Are you all right? You hit your head pretty badly."

"I'm fine. I could've died if you hadn't knocked me out of the way."

"I'm *so* sorry about your place."

"Not your fault." He felt a flash of anger. Those responsible would pay.

"It feels like it is." She hunched her shoulders, dropping back in the seat. "I saw you after. Downstairs, when your friends arrived. You thought I'd done it all. That I'd blown up your place and taken the necklace."

"I was angry. Then I saw the security footage. I saw you foolishly risk your life." He squeezed her fingers. "I saw you save me."

She turned in the seat. "You should forget my name, Zane. Get away and forget I exist."

Fuck, no. He pulled up at the Four Seasons. A very happy valet raced out and took the keys to his car.

Zane took Monroe's arm, keeping a tight grip on her.

"I'm staying here until my place is fixed."

She glanced up at the imposing building, and the flags fluttering overhead. Inside, the lobby was grand, with lots of marble, pillars, and large, live trees. "Of course, you are."

A suited concierge raced over. "Welcome back, Mr. Roth. Can I get you anything?"

133

"No, thank you, Tyler." In the elevator, he swiped his card and they shot upward.

"I'm guessing you have the penthouse," she said.

"Yes. I like being on top."

She rolled her eyes and he fought back a smile.

The door opened straight into the Ty Warner penthouse suite. Zane strode in and dumped his keys on the island.

Monroe made a sound.

The penthouse was on the fifty-second floor, with three-hundred-and-sixty-degree views of New York. The décor consisted of lots of wood, cream fabrics, original artwork, and luxury touches. She walked into the living area. A glass table sat by the large windows, a huge, glass chandelier hanging above it, and the skyscrapers of downtown framed by the window.

"Holy cow. It's like being on top of the world." She turned her head, looking into the adjacent library filled with warm wood, and a grand piano situated by the windows.

He took her hand and pulled her to the couch in front of the fireplace. "Now, talk."

Her gray eyes sparked. "Is that how it works for you? You bark an order and people jump?"

He sat across from her. "Usually."

She gnawed on her lip. "I'm not used to sharing my problems."

"Because I suspect you've had to deal with them by yourself your entire life. Your mother abandoned you, your father was in and out of jail, and you practically raised your younger brother."

Heat filled her cheeks. "Did your PI tell you my favorite brand of underwear, too?"

"You're partial to Victoria's Secret."

"Screw you, Zane."

She went to rise, but he pushed her back down and sat beside her.

"I admire the hell out of you. You've taken care of your brother, started your own successful business."

She just stared at him.

"You're pretty amazing, Monroe."

She closed her eyes. "Be quiet."

"You can't take a compliment. What a surprise."

Her eyes snapped open. "I don't want you hurt. You shouldn't wade into this."

"I'm already in the center of it." He entwined their fingers. "Spill, O'Connor."

"My brother Maguire is in trouble."

Vander's report had already outlined that the young man was a little wild. So it was her brother who was in trouble, not an ex-lover. Zane was relieved.

"He's in debt to the Mafia. Russians."

Fuck. Okay, not so relieved, after all.

She twisted her hands together. "They said I had to steal the Phillips-Morley necklace in payment for his debt."

Zane blew out a breath. "Okay."

"But someone else took it, and the Russians don't care. They want me to get the necklace, or they'll kill Maguire."

Zane squeezed her hand. "We'll get him back."

So many emotions crossed her face.

"You aren't alone, Monroe."

"If you make me cry, I'll get mad."

He smiled. "Right. Let me make a call." He rose and pulled out his cell phone, and thumbed the screen. It rang.

"Norcross."

"I'm with Monroe," Zane said.

"I'm on my way."

Zane turned to her. "My security guy is on the way. We'll come up with a plan of attack. I want the names of the people who attacked my home. I'm not letting them get away with that. We'll get the necklace back, then we'll save your brother."

Her brows drew together. "You'll...you'll hand over the necklace for Mag?"

God, had no one *ever* put her first? "Yes, if I have to."

She pressed her lips together and looked away.

Moments later, he heard the whir of the elevator. The doors opened and Vander stepped out.

He hadn't shaved, and his cheeks were covered in dark stubble. He wore a suit, but it didn't soften his edges.

Monroe's eyes widened. She shifted closer to Zane.

"Monroe O'Connor, Vander Norcross."

"Um, hey," she said.

Vander lifted his chin.

"The Russians are holding Monroe's brother," Zane said.

"Fuck." Vander slipped his hands into his pockets. "Okay, tell me everything."

Vander listened as Monroe ran through what had happened.

"I'll make some calls and see if we can find out where he is, and who's got him." Vander met Zane's gaze.

Zane nodded. "Any word on the thieves who took the necklace?"

"Nothing concrete yet, but it could be linked to a jewelry gang that Rome ran into trouble with back in San Francisco."

Rome Nash was Vander's top bodyguard. The big former Navy SEAL had stoic down to a fine art, and badass stamped all over him.

"How are Rome and his princess?" Zane asked.

Vander's lips quirked. "Princess Sofia brought that man happily to his knees." Vander shook his head like he couldn't quite believe it. "Okay, sit tight. Let me see what intel we can get on all the players."

Monroe nodded, looking a little dazed.

"Thanks, Vander." Zane shook the man's hand and saw him out.

When Zane turned, Monroe was standing at the windows talking on her cell phone.

"You're sure everything's fine at the shop, Chloe? Uh-huh. Okay. Isabella made it in to help you?" A pause. "No, you tell nobody about Zane. All right. Thanks, Chloe, bye."

He could see the tension in Monroe's body. She was tired, and running on fumes.

"Everything okay at the shop."

She glanced at him. "Yes."

"When was the last time you slept?"

"I can't sleep. I worry about Mag, I worry about

stealing from you..." She wrapped her arms around herself.

Zane went to the kitchen, poured a glass of milk, and set it in the microwave. Once it dinged, he carried it over to her.

She eyed it, then sipped it suspiciously. "Milk?"

"It's supposed to be relaxing."

She made a harrumphing sound. "So's whiskey."

"I have Scotch."

She gasped. "Zane, the only whiskey is a good Irish one." Her nose wrinkled. "I don't like milk." But she drank it.

"You need to relax. You're safe here."

"I don't think any woman is safe with you."

She did a slow blink. He took the glass and set it on the coffee table.

"You're too handsome, and too rich," she said.

He circled an arm around her and made her sit on the couch. He moved behind her, lifted his hands to her shoulders, and started massaging.

Her muscles were so tense.

She let out a small moan and her head dropped forward.

"You're too everything," she whispered.

Zane was fucking glad that she was as tangled up as he was.

Right now, he had a driving need to see her rest. "Just relax."

She watched the flickering flames in the fireplace, and it wasn't long before he saw her eyelids droop.

Moments later, she slumped back against him, and he realized she was asleep.

He shifted so he could see her face. She looked relaxed. He touched her cheekbone, and his chest filled with a sensation he didn't recognize.

He scooped her up and she snuggled into him.

Shit.

He strode into the bedroom and lay her on the bed. He stripped off her shoes, then tugged her jeans off.

He studiously avoided looking at the tiny, black panties and those long, long legs.

Then he tucked her in.

Monroe

Oh, there was nothing better than waking up in a soft bed, all snuggly and warm.

I snuggled into the pillow and smiled. It was nice to relax...

Wait.

I sat up and blinked. This room was definitely *not* my cramped bedroom.

No, this room was huge, with a giant bed covered in fancy, cream covers with... I squinted. Was that gold thread?

Shaking my head, I took a second to stare at the gob-smacking view of New York and Central Park through the floor-to-ceiling windows.

Zane. He'd lulled me to sleep like a child.

I leaped out of bed, my blood fizzing. He'd just taken over. My brother was in danger, and I had shit to do.

Then I realized that I wasn't wearing my jeans.

I huffed out a breath. He'd undressed me as well.

That high-handed, bossy billionaire.

I didn't even bother to look for my jeans, and, letting anger fuel me, I stomped into the living area.

"I have a bone to pick with you, Roth."

He was in the library, standing near the grand piano, phone in hand. His gaze flicked to me, then ran down my bare legs.

Traitorous heat knotted in my gut.

"Sounds like you have your hands full, Zane."

Liam Kensington's crisp voice came through the phone speaker. He sounded amused.

"I have my hands full with all you smug, bossy billionaires," I snapped.

Liam's rich laughter sounded. "Talk to you later, pal."

Zane set the phone aside. "I see you woke up on the wrong side of the bed."

"I didn't want to sleep. I have responsibilities and issues to deal with, and a brother to save."

"You needed to rest. You were running on fumes."

I growled. "I've been looking after myself for a long time, Roth."

"You can't help your brother if you can't think straight."

Damn, I hated that he had a point.

"That's not the point," I insisted.

"What is the point? I just encouraged you to relax. I didn't drug you or strap you down." He crossed his arms.

He was wearing a loose, white shirt, with the sleeves rolled up and I was distracted by the bronze skin and corded muscles in his forearms.

"Monroe?"

I blinked. "What?"

His lips quirked. "Why are you pissed off?"

"Because." Shit, my brain was not working.

He stalked toward me. "You're mad because I took care of you?"

Damn. I swallowed. I was mad because no one had ever taken care of me before. I liked it, and I was terrified that I'd get used to it, and then he'd take it away.

There was no happy ending for a bachelor billionaire and me. This wasn't one of those romcoms that Sabrina loved, and forced me to watch on her movie nights.

His hot gaze slid down my legs and he stopped in front of me.

My anger started morphing into something else. Just as hot and volatile.

Damn, I wanted him. Desperately.

And right now, right here, he was standing right in front of me.

Maybe I could soak in enough of him to last me a lifetime once he was gone.

Why the hell not? I grabbed the front of his shirt and yanked him closer. Surprise flared in his eyes.

Then I went on my toes and kissed him.

The kiss was rough and reckless. Red-hot desire fizzed in my belly as our mouths ate at each other. He made a deep sound in the back of his throat that vibrated through me.

Yes, yes, yes. Panic, excitement, desperation, it all burst inside me.

"Jesus," he muttered.

I attacked the buttons on his shirt. *Shit.* Why was it so hard to get the buttons open? I needed skin. *Screw it.* I gripped the shirt and yanked.

Buttons pinged across the marble tiles.

Zane growled and backed me up.

I pressed my mouth to his chest. I kissed, licked, and nipped his skin. "I love your body."

"I feel the same way about yours."

His heart was racing, and a pulse of need throbbed between my legs. I'd made this sexy man's heart race. Me, Monroe O'Connor.

Then our lips clashed again. I moaned, and his hands kneaded my ass. *Yes.*

"Touch me," I panted.

"I am."

He ripped my shirt off, and a second later, my bra was gone. Then his palms covered my breasts, and I arched into him.

"Look at these pretty nipples." He bent me over his arm and then his mouth was on me.

Oh, *oh.* Frantically, I groped for him. I had one hand in his dark hair, the other clenched on his hard bicep.

My nipple turned to a hard nub between his teeth, then he found the other one. He dragged me to the floor, kicking his pants and boxers off.

Yes. Need for him was wild inside me.

"Zane. Please. *Now.*"

"God, hearing you beg makes me even harder."

I caught his cock and stroked.

"Not yet." He pulled my hand away, then stripped my panties off.

I was mindless, frantic for him. I scratched my nails down his arms.

"Patience, little Wildcat."

He knelt between my legs, then gripped my hips, his hands under my ass. He lifted me to his mouth.

God. *Oh, God.*

He ate me like he was starving. His tongue stabbed inside me and I moaned, arching up. That mouth...

He slid my legs over his shoulders with a growl.

"*Zane!*"

"You taste so fucking good, Monroe." He lapped at me and I dug my heels into his back.

I needed to get closer. I needed more of that mouth of his.

My climax was bearing down on me like a speeding train. I was making incoherent noises.

He pulled me closer, his stubble scraping sensitive places.

My orgasm hit hard. I screamed.

All thoughts were gone, and there was only sensation pouring through me.

"*Zane!*"

With a final lap, he lifted his head. His face was taut with desire, his eyes glowing. "We haven't finished yet."

13

WILDCAT

Zane

If he didn't have her, he was going to lose his mind.

Right then and there, with Monroe beneath him, her husky cries echoing in his ears, and the taste of her on his lips, Zane needed her. He wanted her more than he'd wanted anything in his life. He fumbled for his wallet and found a condom.

She watched him as he rolled it on, her lips parted.

He surged over her and took her mouth with his. He knew she'd taste her own sweet muskiness.

With a moan, she kissed him back, wild like the wind. She wound her arms and legs around him. He dragged the head of his cock through her wetness, anticipation making it hard to breathe.

"Do it," she pleaded. "Fuck me, Zane."

He slid into her with one hard thrust.

Heat. Tightness. Wet.

"*Fuck*, Monroe."

Her body clenched on him and he heard her panting.

"You fit me," she breathed.

"I'm buried in you. Shit." Zane pulled back and thrust again. He savored the feeling of being connected to her.

Their gazes locked. She held on tight, and they moved faster.

"Zane," she whimpered. "Harder."

He thrust harder. The final strands of his restraint broke.

His. He drove deep, his hips bucking against hers, his cock driving deep.

Zane felt a primal need to stamp his ownership on her. He couldn't get close enough, deep enough. She met each stroke, hips lifting up, and her cries filling the air.

Her nails raked down his back.

"Come," he growled. "Fuck, Wildcat." He tilted his hips. "Come for me."

Her inner muscles clenched on his cock. She let out a sharp cry, her body shuddering under the pleasure.

His own orgasm burst through him, ramming down his spine. With a grunt, his thrusts lost any semblance of rhythm.

He shoved his face in her neck, then bit down hard.

Her body spasmed again, then he slumped on her, sucking in harsh breaths.

Hell. He'd emptied himself inside her, yet he felt full. Like all the emptiness inside him was gone.

Dazed, he dragged in a breath and sat back.

She was sprawled on the tiles, her lips parted, and her eyes closed.

Shit, he'd fucked her on the floor. He'd been rough, a damn animal. He could see the mark on her neck from where he'd bit her.

His gut clenched.

Then those gray eyes opened and she smiled. "Roth, you sure know how to show a girl a good time."

"You okay?"

"Oh, I'm about a thousand levels above okay." She tugged his head down and kissed him.

He relaxed, cupping one of her breasts. "Your heart's still racing."

Her smile widened. "I'm surprised it's still beating. I was afraid it had stopped. I might need you to check my legs, though, as I can't feel them."

Smiling, he slid his hands down her legs. He stroked her thighs and then behind her knees.

She shivered and giggled. Such a sweet sound that he'd never expected to hear from her.

"Ms. O'Connor, I do believe there is sensation in your legs."

"It's a miracle, Dr. Roth."

He pressed a quick kiss to her shoulder. "I meant to be gentle, and show you my best moves."

She arched a dark brow. "If those are your worst ones, we're both in trouble."

"Don't move." He rose.

She shot a hot glance at his naked body. "I can't move, even if I wanted to."

Zane strode to the half bath and dealt with the condom. When he got back to her, that gorgeous body was still stretched out on the tiles.

He slid his arms around her, lifted her, and carried her into the bedroom.

He set her on the bed and watched her gaze slide up his body.

His cock responded.

She smiled. "Good to see that lazy, rich billionaires have some stamina."

"Lazy?" He tweaked her nipple. "I work out several times a week, I'll have you know."

With a laugh, she rolled and sat up on the edge of the bed.

His hardening cock was right in front of her face. She licked her lips.

Zane groaned, sensation flaring deep in his gut. "You want my cock, Wildcat?"

She nodded. He slid a hand into her hair, not directing, just anchoring. With his other hand, he circled his cock.

He ran the swollen head across her lips and her tongue darted out. She made a hungry sound.

"Fuck," he ground. "You want more of me, Monroe?"

She nodded.

"Open that sweet mouth."

She did, then she sucked him deep.

Zane lost his grip on his control, pleasure driving through him.

She moaned on his cock, sucking hard. She pressed her hands to his thighs, her fingers digging in. He felt his cock swell. Watching her suck his cock was too damned good.

He wasn't going to last much longer in that sweet mouth.

He pulled back. "I want to come inside you."

"*Yes.*"

"Condom." He gestured to the table beside the bed.

She opened the bedside table, tore open a packet, then gripped his cock.

He locked his legs as she rolled it on. *Damn*. It took all his control to stay still.

Then she scooted back on the bed, sliding a hand between her thighs.

Fuck. So sexy and beautiful. "Play with that clit, Wildcat. Feel good?"

She writhed; her face flushed. "Yes."

He climbed on the bed, his back to the headboard. "Come here, Monroe."

She crawled toward him, her eyes alight, her lips pink from being stretched around his cock. She straddled him, her hands cupping his shoulders.

When the tip of his cock slid through her slick folds, they both groaned. She spread her thighs and sank down.

"*Oh.*" Her teeth sank into her bottom lip. "You feel so good stretching me, Zane."

Shit. "Yeah." He gripped her hips and forced her down. "Take all of me."

She sank all the way down and moaned his name.

"Now ride me. I'm not going to last long."

She gripped his shoulders, her hips rising and falling.

Beauty. Pure beauty.

"You're mine, my little thief." He cupped her breasts. "These are mine. Your pussy's mine. You're all mine."

"Barbarian," she panted.

He never had been before. Only with her.

His thumb found her clit, and she shuddered. "Oh, God."

Zane bucked his hips up. She stiffened, then screamed his name.

As she came, he pumped deep, her body clenching on his cock.

He yanked her closer, then his own release hit.

Zane poured himself inside her, holding her tight.

Monroe

I opened my eyes and saw abs.

Delicious, gorgeous abs covered in bronze skin. Maybe I was still dreaming. Dreaming of a hot, male body wasn't so bad.

Especially when they smelled good too.

Today was Tuesday, which was the one day of the week that I got to sleep in. Sabrina opened the store on Tuesdays, and I went in later.

As I shifted my legs in the sheets, I felt a twinge between my thighs. I stilled.

Then I lifted my head and saw a beautiful flaccid cock resting on a hard thigh.

Uh-oh. I remembered the first time I'd seen that cock, while slipping around in a bathroom.

Oh, hell. I'd sucked that cock. And ridden it. And—

I sat upright.

"You going to lose your shit?"

The deep murmur made my head swivel.

My breath caught.

Zane looked edible. He was lying naked, diagonal on the bed. The bed was a mess from our wild, energetic night together. I'd woken him once. He'd woken me twice. The covers were torn off and pillows were missing.

"I'm thinking about it." Shit, I'd slept with Zane Roth.

Correction—we'd fucked each other's brains out. Multiple times.

There hadn't been much sleeping.

Suddenly, he grabbed me, and I found myself plastered against his bare body.

"Zane—"

"Don't lose it. It was good, Monroe. Beyond good." He nipped my lips. "Totally hot, sexy, and delicious."

God, my insides were melting.

"My life is a hot mess," I said.

He grinned. "A hot, sexy mess." He cupped my breast and toyed with the nipple.

"That's not helping," I moaned. I was wet in an instant.

"I'm distracting you from having a meltdown." His mouth closed over my nipple.

Oh, God, I was so weak.

He turned me and pushed me down on my belly. His lips traveled down my spine.

I writhed. I loved his hands and mouth on me.

He reached my buttocks, kneaded. I made a hungry sound.

Then I heard the crinkle of a wrapper. He lifted my hips, and surged inside me.

"*Zane.*" So good. So deep.

"Fuck, I love the way you say my name."

I pressed my cheek to the sheet, my body shuddering under each thrust.

"Take me, Monroe."

"I'll take whatever you give me."

He growled.

I felt his hand snake under my body, then his fingers rubbed my clit. On his next thrust, I splintered apart, coming hard.

I moaned helplessly as he pumped inside me one last time. He ground against me, groaning as he came.

He collapsed on top of me and nuzzled my hair. I heard the harsh pants of his breath.

"Wildcat." He kissed the back of my neck.

"Zane."

"Hmm, nothing better than having my cock inside you when you murmur my name."

"Well, I'm feeling too good to freak out now."

"Good." He stroked my back, then pulled out.

I stayed sprawled there, mellowed, as he disappeared into the bathroom. I sighed. I'd save my freakout for later.

He sauntered out, naked and gorgeous. I drank him in and sighed again.

"Do you need to get to your store?" he asked.

I shook my head. "Sabrina opens today."

"Hungry?" he asked.

For all kinds of things. "I could eat."

He sat on the bed and grabbed the phone off the

bedside table. As he ordered room service, I watched him wince and rub his neck.

"What's wrong with your neck?" I asked, once he'd hung up.

"I wrenched it when a sexy brunette knocked me out of the way of a bomb blast."

I sat up. "Lie down."

He raised a brow.

"Come on, Roth. I won't hurt you."

He lay facedown on the bed, and I swallowed. He had a sexy back, all corded muscle.

Not to mention his ass. Pure poetry.

I straddled him, and started massaging his neck and shoulders.

He groaned and I smiled. I kept kneading.

"You're good at this."

"I did a massage course a few years ago. Before I started the shop. I needed the work." I'd worked three jobs for a while.

He moaned again. Such a small thing, but I liked taking care of him. He was a man who had everything, or could get it, if he wanted it. It was nice to be able to do something for him.

I worked on a knot and got another long groan.

I leaned over him. "Do you like that? Does it feel good?"

With a growl, he rolled, pinning me under him.

"I do like it. I like you."

My gaze locked with his. My chest filled with warmth. "Zane..."

The doorbell rang.

Something rippled across his face. "That'll be break-fast." He levered up and reached for a pair of loose, black pants resting over a chair. "Get dressed, Wildcat."

By the time I'd pulled on one of Zane's T-shirts, he was wheeling a trolley in. He lifted silver lids and the glorious smell of bacon and fresh pastry made my mouth water.

"I'm starving," I said.

"I'm not surprised."

He handed me a glass of juice. I loaded up a plate with pastries and bacon, and put a few slices of fruit on it for my health's sake. I sat cross-legged in the center of the bed.

"So, you practically raised your brother?" he said.

I took a bite of pastry and nodded. "Mag doesn't remember his mom." Even I only had vague memories of a soft voice and nervous hands. My own mother was an even dimmer memory. She liked to shout and slap. "My mother left when I was four. Then Da met Mag's mom. She was nice to me. She and my da fought a lot. Aileen was...nervous. Dad always had a con running." I shrugged. "Eventually, she couldn't cope with the stress of it."

A dark look settled on Zane's face. "So, she abandoned you and her kid? Let you deal with it?"

I shrugged again. "I don't think of her or my mom much. Da is far from perfect, but as kids, we always had food on the table, and clothes to wear." I didn't mention that he'd leave us alone, sometimes for days. "I looked after Mag. Packed his bag, got us to school, and helped him with homework."

"That's damn impressive, Monroe."

"I just did what any sister would do. Tried to keep life normal. Survived." I wrinkled my nose. "An aunt helped when dad was sent to jail, until I turned eighteen." My belly twisted, old memories filling my head. It was damn scary to be a teenager, and to know you needed to feed and protect your baby brother.

"My dad left when I was seven," Zane said.

My heart clenched. Some part of me had imagined that rich people led charmed lives. "I'm sorry."

"It was just mom and me. She worked two jobs, but she still baked cookies and came to my football games."

"She sounds wonderful."

"She is. The necklace was for her. She's always been fascinated by it."

The pastry turned to dust in my mouth. I grabbed his hand. "God, Zane, I'm so sorry—"

"It's not your fault."

"I'm so angry at Maguire." I picked up a cube of watermelon. "He's forced me to break vows that I made to myself. To never use the skills my father taught me for harm."

"Hey." Zane cupped my cheeks. "You are *not* your father."

"For a while, I was. He taught me to pick a pocket, to pick a lock, to crack a safe." I swallowed. "When I was younger, he took me on jobs when he needed someone small."

Zane's face twisted, something dark flashing in his eyes. "He took you on jobs?"

Ashamed, I nodded. "At first, I was too young to

understand. It was just a fun game." I tucked a strand of hair back. "Then I worked out stealing from other people was illegal and wrong. He'd praise me, was proud of me, so for a while, I still went along with it."

Zane's hand cupped the back of my neck. "He was an adult, your father. He manipulated you."

"I know." But it didn't always make me feel better.

"What happened?"

"I guess all the taunts from the kids at school started to seep in. The smug looks, the sneers, the jibes. Everyone knew my father was a criminal. Then he stole from the family of a boy from school. The father owned a trucking business." My stomach lurched. "I cracked the safe. Da cleaned out all the cash." Old shame burned my veins like acid.

Zane kept rubbing my neck. He wasn't pulling away in disgust, just offering me quiet support.

I blew out a breath. "The business went bankrupt. The boy's father committed suicide, and I was there the day they came to get him from class to tell him. I saw him...crumple."

"It's not your fault, Monroe, you were a child."

I met his gaze. "That day, I vowed never to steal. Never to use what he taught me to harm others."

"And now you run a business to help people make their homes safe and secure. You volunteer at a shelter to help women who've been preyed on feel safe. You share information on your blog and socials on locks and alarms."

Jeez, Vander really dug deep when he investigated someone. "I'm not a saint, Zane."

"No, but you're also definitely not your father, Monroe."

I nodded. I wanted to believe him.

"And we're going to steal the necklace back," he said. "Together."

I just stared at him. I'd never been part of a couple. Or a team. I'd always been solo.

"We're going to save your brother," he said.

I desperately wanted to believe him.

14

WHAT'S THE PLAN?

Zane

Zane loved watching Monroe eat. She did it with gusto, and when she licked her fingers, it gave him ideas.

"Coffee?" he asked.

"*Mmm,*" she moaned. "Yes, please."

The moan gave him ideas too.

After a night of exclusive access to that long body, and some very enthusiastic fucking, his damn cock shouldn't be so eager.

He poured a coffee and handed her a mug. She drank it with glee.

He suspected Monroe O'Connor did everything with enthusiasm. Would she love someone like that, too?

His gut tightened. She clearly loved her screwup brother.

Zane's cell phone rang, and he thumbed the button. "Vander."

"I'm on my way to you. I've got news."

"Good. See you soon."

Zane met Monroe's gaze, and watched as she gnawed her lip.

"What if we can't get the necklace?" she said. "God, what if they kill Mag?"

Zane yanked her into his arms. "Not going to happen. You aren't alone anymore, remember?"

She gave him a small nod. When she held on tight, he savored it.

"Go take a shower and change. I don't need Vander seeing those legs of yours."

"That man is hot, but he's scary."

"Yeah, he probably knows ten thousand ways to kill a man." Zane tapped her nose. "Go."

Her voice lowered. "Going to join me?"

"No, or Vander will get to hear the screams you make when you come."

Her nose wrinkled. "You're pretty sure of yourself, Roth."

"Yep." He kissed her nose.

"And cocky."

"Especially when you're around."

"More than a little arrogant."

"I like to think confident."

She rose and he slapped her butt.

Once she was in the shower, he showered in the guest bathroom. Afterward, he pulled on a blue polo and jeans.

When Monroe strode out of the bedroom, back in her jeans, but wearing one of his white business shirts, she looked ridiculously good. Her dark hair was damp, and tied up in a messy knot.

She stumbled to a halt, staring at him.

"What?" he asked.

"I've never seen you in jeans. I didn't know billionaires wore jeans." She squinted. "Are they Armani?"

"No." They were Gucci, but he wasn't telling her that. "I'm just a person, regardless of my work, or how much money I have in my bank accounts."

She walked toward him. "I know, but Zane, there is a huge gulf between you and me."

"Bullshit."

She huffed out a breath. "I'm the daughter of a criminal. A con man, a thief. And any zeroes in my bank account are after the decimal point."

"And I told you before, I'm the son of a man who abandoned his wife and son. We are who we make ourselves. We aren't the sins of our parents."

"Damn, you're stubborn."

"I was thinking the same thing about you." He yanked her to him. As soon as his mouth touched hers, desire flared.

And damned if he didn't feel like getting burned.

He pulled her up on her toes and she threw her arms around his neck. When she moaned, his cock pressed hard against the zipper of his jeans.

He wanted her with a need that bordered on madness.

A throat clearing made Zane lift his head.

Vander stood there, dressed all in black—black jeans,

black Henley, and a black leather jacket. Shit, Zane hadn't even heard the elevator.

Monroe squeaked and pulled back. Zane held her in place, pinned against him. She tried to break free again, then shot him a look.

The man's dark-blue eyes took them in, scanned over Monroe wearing Zane's shirt, and his lips quirked. "Morning."

"Coffee?" Zane nudged Monroe toward the couch.

When Vander lifted his chin, Zane poured the man a mug of black coffee.

As the men sat, Monroe jumped up and started pacing. Nervous tension pumped off her.

"I confirmed that your brother is being held by a man called Pavel Sidorov," Vander said. "He's high up in the Russian mafia here in New York. Not a good guy to be in debt to."

Monroe froze, her face turning white.

Zane tugged her down beside him, and wrapped an arm around her shoulders. She grabbed his hand and held on tight.

"I also arranged to meet with Sidorov." Vander sipped his coffee.

"You can do that?" Monroe asked.

"I can and I did. We met this morning. I let Sidorov know I'd entered the scene on behalf of Monroe. Sidorov doesn't know me, but knows of me."

And the man would know that you wouldn't want to piss Vander Norcross off.

"I saw your brother," Vander continued. "He is fine, and they haven't hurt him."

Releasing a breath, Monroe sagged against Zane. "Thank God."

"The necklace has a link to some ancestor of Sidorov's. He is obsessed with it. He's given us extra time to get it back."

Zane would find some other gift for his mother. He wasn't giving her anything that some mobster wanted.

"That brings us to who stole the necklace." Vander set his coffee mug on the table, then pulled out three photos. He lined them up on the table. They were clearly taken with long-distance lenses, and the people in them had no idea.

They all looked younger than Zane. Good-looking. Wearing designer clothes.

"Do you recognize any of them?" Vander asked.

Monroe shook her head.

"These are the men who were in Zane's penthouse. My tech guy, Ace, tracked them down fast because they are linked to the jewelry gang that Rome just busted up in San Francisco called the Black Foxes. The gang is comprised of disenfranchised European aristocracy, to which our three thieves here belong." Vander stabbed a finger at a dark-haired man. "This guy's a prince, with a fondness for parties, women, and racing cars. Prince Franz of Saxe-Bavaria. He's related to some aristocratic German family. His side of the family are low on funds."

"Wait." Zane frowned. "That name's familiar. He tried to get a meeting with me. To pitch me some project to invest in."

"Maybe a way to get close to you, then get into your penthouse and take a look around." Vander pointed to the next picture. "Jean-Baptiste Bissette is French. Owns a crumbling family château in the south of France, and needs money to restore it. And Leonardo Alamanni is Italian, and from what Ace dug up, he's got money, but he's just an asshole. He's a trust-fund baby who likes the thrill of stealing."

Zane glared at the pictures. These men could have killed him and Monroe, all for money and kicks.

"They attended the charity auction where you bought the necklace, Zane. They were likely scouting for a target."

"They're not getting away with this."

Vander gave him a faint smile. "No, they aren't."

"What's the plan?" Monroe asked.

"The trio rented a place on the Upper East Side, near Central Park. My guess is they have the necklace stashed there. They'll be at a new nightclub-opening tonight as special guests. Club Real. Real as in Spanish word for royal."

"Like Real Madrid," Zane murmured.

Vander nodded. "They're going to be the star euro-trash royalty attractions. My plan is to visit their rental house and look for the necklace."

"When you say visit," Monroe said, "you mean break and enter."

"I'm not planning to break anything," Vander said dryly. "If I can't find the necklace, I'll leave a bug and listen in."

Monroe rose. "I'm coming."

"What?" Zane shot to his feet. "No way."

"Yes. I'm good at this." She met Vander's gaze. "And

if there's a safe, I can crack it."

Zane cursed. "No."

Vander sipped the last of his coffee. "She does have skills."

"Fuck."

"It's my brother's life. I'm coming."

Zane gritted his teeth. "Then I'm coming, too."

Monroe

I swiped the lipstick across my lips. A bright give-me-sex-now red.

Next, I settled the wig on my head. This one was bright-red, in a long bob style that brushed my shoulders. I was still in my lingerie, in my tiny bathroom in my apartment above Lady Locksmith.

After my morning with Zane and Vander, Zane had dropped me back at my place on his way to his office. I'd snuck upstairs, changed, then gone to the shop for a few hours of work in the back room. I'd deftly avoided any interrogations from Sabrina, and thankfully, it appeared that Chloe had kept quiet about Zane. A teenage girl who could keep a secret, who knew.

Dragging in a deep breath, I looked at myself in the mirror. My eyes were smoky, dark, and sexy. The first part of tonight's plan was for me to attend the Club Real opening, and confirm that Prince Franz, Bissette, and Alamanni were there.

Vander took nothing at face value and left nothing to

chance. I'd watched the man plan tonight's mission with exhausting detail. The guy could seriously plan the invasion of a small country without breaking a sweat.

I hated that Zane was coming on this B and E expedition.

If we were caught...

I rubbed my temple. I had it so bad for him.

With a shake of my head, I strode into my bedroom... to find Zane sprawled on my queen-size bed.

He looked out of place and larger-than-life in my small room.

His hungry gaze roamed over me. "I like your outfit."

I rolled my eyes. "I don't know how you make billions when you have sex on the brain all the time."

"It's only when I look at you that I have sex on the brain." He sat up and glanced at my bedside table. "I like your clock. I don't think we've done nine o'clock."

"See, sex on the brain." I opened my closet and several things fell out.

Gah, I'd been meaning to tidy it. It wasn't that I had that many clothes, it was just that the closet was tiny. I'd already packed a small bag of B and E clothes to change into later. I couldn't break into a house in this microscopic dress.

I yanked the dress out and slithered into it. It was covered in dangly, silver sequins. The thing barely covered my butt, and had tiny straps that left my shoulders mostly bare.

Next, I dug around in my closet and pulled out my strappy silver heels. I pulled them on and turned.

Zane scowled at me. "Don't you have another dress?

That's longer? With more fabric?"

I finished fastening the strap on my shoe. "Why don't you thump your chest? Me Tarzan, you Jane."

In a fast move, he snaked an arm around me. "Me Zane, you mine."

My heart skipped a beat. "Neanderthal."

"I don't want you doing this. I don't want you going into that nightclub alone, or breaking into this house."

"I don't want you on this job either, so we're even."

He lowered his head.

"Don't ruin my lipstick!"

He brushed my lips lightly.

"No unnecessary risks tonight, Monroe. In, out, and don't get hurt."

Some hard, protected part of me melted. "Same, Roth."

We left my apartment. Out on the street, a sleek, black BMW X6 pulled up, Vander in the driver's seat.

Zane and I climbed in the back.

"Ready?" Vander looked in the rearview mirror.

"No," Zane said.

"Yes," I said.

It didn't take long to pull up at the nightclub in Chelsea. I saw a long line waiting out on the sidewalk.

"Here." Vander leaned back. He held a necklace in his hand. It was choker-style, with a shiny pendant in the center.

"It's got a microphone. We'll be able to hear what you say. Get in, confirm the three men are present and settled, and get out."

I nodded and fastened the choker around my neck.

Zane yanked me in for a hard, deep kiss. My head spun. He tasted so addictive.

When he pulled back, his lips were smudged red.

I rubbed them with my thumb. "See you soon, Roth."

I opened the door, slipped out, and sauntered toward the front of the line and the entrance to Club Real.

The line was long, but when the bouncer saw me coming, his eyes lit with appreciation.

He lifted the rope and I walked by him with a smile.

Inside the nightclub was dark, with lots of touches of red. Huge, brocade wall hangings covered the walls.

"For the opening, everyone needs a sexy face mask." The hostess at the front handed me a sparkly, Mardi Gras-style mask, with sequins and feathers. I slipped it on.

The dance floor was crowded, the bars were busy, and every table and seat were filled. Lights strobed across the dance floor. Several female dancers, clad only in glittery mesh outfits with tiaras on their heads, danced provocatively on raised platforms.

"I'm in," I murmured.

It didn't have quite the classy vibe of Liam Kensington's club, Mayfair. Club Real was a little too overblown and in your face. I skirted the dance floor and scanned faces, searching for the men. The masks didn't make it easy.

There.

One of the men—Bissette—was standing at a high drinks table with not one, but two women draped all over him. He smiled, kissed one of the women, then the other.

Ew.

"Bissette is at a table." I pivoted and walked through the tables. I dodged several men who tried to talk to me.

Come on. The others had to be here.

"Ladies and gentlemen," the DJ yelled. "I hope you're loving Club Real!"

Applause and shouts erupted.

"Here, we can all be royalty for the night. We also have some real royals here to open the club. Prince Franz is cutting some moves on the dance floor."

I swiveled. There were more cheers and applause, and I moved to the edge of the dance floor.

Oh, boy. The prince was dancing with a woman.

Dirty dancing.

They were grinding against each other and he bent her back, groins mashed together. He slid his hand up her tiny skirt.

Charming.

"Franz is on the dance floor," I murmured.

Next, I headed to the crowded bar. Leaning against it, I searched the shadows. *Two down, one to go.*

"Hello," an accented voice drawled.

I lifted my head.

Bingo.

Leonardo Alamanni leaned over me. His mask was gold and ornate, but it was clearly him. He had dark, curly hair, and dark-bronze skin.

"You are the most beautiful creature here."

I managed to keep a straight face. He probably thought the accent made him instantly sexy. It didn't.

"Can I buy you a drink?" he asked.

I smiled. "No."

He blinked, looking a bit shocked.

I turned away. Once he left, I could leave. This asshole had planted a bomb. He'd stolen the necklace, and he could've killed Zane.

Anger was a hot spurt in my veins, but I bit my tongue.

"But it would be my pleasure." Alamanni ran a finger down my arm. "And I could make it your pleasure, *bella*."

What a waste of space. He could use his looks and his brain, and work to add to the world instead of taking away from it. Instead, he was indulged, and stole what wasn't his.

"Take your hand off me, or I'll break your fingers," I drawled.

He froze. I watched lust flare in his eyes.

What was wrong with this guy?

"I like a woman with fire. *Il incendio*."

Ugh. I rolled my eyes. "Go away."

"I can't. I've been struck by your beauty."

Wow, I was shocked that this guy ever got laid.

"Is there an angry boyfriend I should be worried about?" he asked. "Is that what's holding you back, *bella*?"

Because me saying no wasn't a deterrent. I mentally rolled my eyes. "Yes, my..." boyfriend was way too juvenile "...man would be very, very unhappy."

Alamanni's hand moved across the bar, and trailed over my hand. "I think you'd be worth the hassle."

A hard body pressed in behind me. A fist slammed on the bar...right on top of Alamanni's hand. He yelped.

"The lady told you to leave her alone."

Zane's icy tone promised bloodshed.

Damn him. He shouldn't be in here. If anyone recognized him...

I turned and pressed into him. He had a simple black half-mask over his face. "Hey, honey bear."

God, he smelled good. I glanced at Alamanni. "I call him honey bear because he's usually as sweet as honey, but when he gets riled...he's as angry as a bear."

Alamanni muttered under his breath.

"Go," Zane growled. "Before I break your hand for touching her."

With a sniff, Alamanni whirled and stalked away.

"I could have dealt with him," I hissed under my breath.

"Come on." Keeping a tight hold on my hand, he towed me toward the door. People flew out of his way.

"It was stupid of you to come in here. If someone recognizes you—"

"I wasn't going to let the asshole—"

"No." I squeezed Zane's hand. "*I* wasn't going to let him do anything. I can take care of myself, Roth."

In the small entry, he pulled me close and ripped our masks off. Our faces were inches apart.

"Well, you have me taking care of you now, too. Get used to it."

Confusing emotions filled me, and I swallowed. "No one ever has."

His face softened, and his palm cupped my cheek. "Then you'd better get used to it, fast."

He pulled me outside.

The black SUV pulled up, and he tugged me in.

15

___

YOUR LUCKY NIGHT

Zane

In the backseat, Zane tried to stare out the window as Vander drove them to the Upper East Side.

This was torture.

Monroe had just slithered out of that poor excuse for a dress. She was right beside him, pulling on tight leggings and a fitted, long-sleeve top. She twisted, and he had the perfect view of her panty-clad ass.

He couldn't resist a quick touch.

"Hey." She looked back over one slim shoulder and shot him a look.

Those eyes and red lips...

He desperately wanted her. She fascinated him, challenged him. He realized now how much he'd gotten used to people always telling him what they thought he wanted to hear. Most people never disagreed with him.

He only trusted Liam, Mav, and his mom to give him things straight.

And Vander never sugarcoated anything.

Vander pulled to a stop and parked. Zane peered at the darkness of Central Park ahead.

The three of them got out of the SUV, and Vander slid the keys into his pocket. Next, the security expert shouldered a small backpack. Monroe pulled out a small pack as well, and slid it on her shoulder. It held her safe-cracking gear.

Zane felt underprepared for this breaking and entering. They walked quickly and quietly down the street.

"There it is." Vander nodded his head across the street.

Zane took in the four-story house. It was a French Renaissance mansion just off Fifth Avenue, cream with touches of black, including steps sweeping up to an ornate, black double door.

"There's a terrace out back," Vander said. "That'll be our entry point."

They continued on and turned left on the next street and circled back. Thankfully, while Fifth Avenue was busy, the side streets were quieter at this time of night.

Finally, Vander stopped.

Zane looked up and stiffened. "That terrace is *three* stories up." Plants and foliage were overflowing on the tiny space.

Vander unzipped his backpack and shoved a set of gloves at Zane, then another pair at Monroe.

"Oh, these are Arc'teryx climbing gloves," she said excitedly. "I've always wanted a pair, but they're so expensive."

Zane pulled on the thin, black gloves, touching the

rubber grips on the fingertips and palm. He'd used them before in the gym. He made a note to buy a pair for Monroe.

She touched his arm. "This is going to be a tricky climb. Maybe you should stay—"

"I'm coming," he growled.

"Zane." She huffed out a breath. "You aren't prepared for this."

"I know how to climb, Monroe. Mav, Liam, and I climb every week in the gym."

"Oh." She looked like she was searching for another reason he shouldn't go with her.

"I'm coming, end of story."

She lowered her voice. "I just don't want you to get hurt, or get caught."

Fuck. He kissed her.

"If you two are done." Vander pulled out a small device and aimed it upward. He fired it. A thin rope with a hook on the end flew up with a muffled thump. The hook flew over the ledge of the terrace.

Vander tugged on the small rope, then looked around. A second later, he pressed one boot to the wall and started climbing.

The man moved like a damn spider.

Monroe dragged in a breath. "He makes that look easy."

"You next," Zane said.

He watched her grip the rope and press her feet to the wall. She took a moment to find her rhythm, then climbed up.

Next, Zane took the rope. It didn't seem thick enough to hold his weight, but knowing Vander, it was made from some high-tech material. He was about to climb, when he heard voices approaching.

Shit. He let the rope go and hoped no one would notice it. He pulled out his phone and wandered down the street.

"Yes, I need those contracts tomorrow," he said, improvising.

A couple drew closer, arm in arm.

"No, not good enough," Zane barked into the phone. "We'll have to meet tomorrow."

They passed by, barely sparing him a glance.

Zane released his breath and slipped the phone away.

He moved back to the thin rope and then climbed up. It was tougher than climbing in the gym, but he was grateful for every hour he'd spent climbing and working out.

He pulled himself over the edge.

"Jeez, that was close." Monroe hugged him.

"Pull the rope up," Vander ordered.

Zane gripped it and pulled, hand over hand. He left it coiled on the terrace.

Vander was at the French doors, with a lock pick in hand.

"Security system?" Zane asked.

"Already disabled."

"He is *really* good," Monroe murmured.

The doors opened, and Vander slipped inside. Zane and Monroe followed him.

"The safe is in the library, down one level." Vander's flashlight let out a narrow beam of light.

They were in a large living area, decorated with a nod to the historic feel of the house. The ceiling was carved and ornate, as was the large fireplace. A rug covered the floorboards, and large, framed paintings hung on the walls. There were several uncomfortable-looking, French-style couches, and a well-stocked, built-in bar off to the side.

They moved down the curving staircase, made of gleaming wood. A skylight above would drench the place with light during the day.

"This way." Vander led them into the library.

Wooden shelves covered the walls and were loaded with books. The furniture was all dark wood, paired with burgundy leather.

"The safe should be..." Vander studied the wall of books intently.

The shelves were packed with books of different sizes and colors. Zane saw everything from recent thrillers, to old first editions.

Vander touched a shelf.

Click.

Part of the shelves opened up.

It revealed a safe sitting inside.

Monroe crouched. "It's a Honeywell. Pretty simple."

She opened her backpack and pulled out some tools. Then she lost herself in her work.

Zane crossed his arms over his chest. Damn, it was sexy watching her. She stroked the safe, listening to it, frowning. He was pretty sure she'd completely forgotten he was there beside her.

Next, she pulled out a small drill and lined it up. It whirred as it cut into the metal. She set the drill back in her bag and pulled out a long piece of black cord. When she plugged one end of it into her phone, he realized it was a flexible scope with a camera on the other end.

"Come on, girl." Monroe fed the scope into her newly drilled hole.

Shit, Zane was getting hard watching her.

She watched the small screen and turned the dial.

Click.

Monroe grinned. "Got it."

Zane yanked her up and kissed her. She grinned at him, then turned back and opened the safe.

Then Zane frowned.

Her face fell. "No."

"Fuck," Vander muttered.

The safe was completely empty.

"Is there another safe?" she asked hopefully.

"Not in the house plans," Vander replied. "Let's search the place."

Monroe quickly stowed her gear in her back pack, then pressed a small black patch over the hole she'd drilled.

"It'll make it less obvious, but someone will notice eventually." She closed the safe up and pushed the shelves closed over it.

They moved through the library. Zane checked all the book shelves, while Monroe ran her palms over the walls. Vander crouched, checking the floorboards.

No safe. No necklace.

Vander searched the ground floor, while Monroe and Zane went up to the bedrooms. In one, they waded through empty condom wrappers, discarded clothes, and used towels.

"Pigs," she muttered.

There was no secondary safe. No necklace.

"Where the hell is it?" she said.

Zane heard the worry in her voice. He gripped her shoulders. "We aren't giving up. We'll find it." He touched her jaw.

She nodded.

They met Vander on the stairs, but the man shook his head.

"I'm going to place a bug in the library. Hopefully, we'll get lucky enough to hear where they've stashed it."

Zane gave him a nod.

"I hope Mag's okay." Monroe bit her lip, her face mostly in shadow. "He hasn't got things together, but he's my brother. He's all I've got."

"We'll get him back." Zane cupped her cheeks. "And he's not all you've got. Not anymore."

"Zane." Her gaze fell to his mouth.

He leaned in and kissed her.

Vander reappeared suddenly, and Zane jerked. The man moved like a ghost.

Vander cocked his head. "It's done. Let's—"

There was a noise downstairs. The three of them froze.

Zane heard the front door swing open, followed by voices in the front entry.

"Come on, ladies." An accented drawl. "Come upstairs, and I'll show you how a prince fucks."

The statement was followed by feminine giggles.

Monroe grimaced.

"Let's move," Vander whispered.

They hurried up the stairs and headed into the living room bordering the terrace. Laughter followed them up the stairs.

"Wait," Franz said. "There's more champagne in the bar fridge. I'll get it."

Shit. Zane's gaze crossed to the built-in bar.

In the room where they were standing.

There was no time to get out onto the terrace and over the ledge. Vander waved a hand at them, and literally disappeared into the shadows.

"Here." Zane yanked Monroe down behind the couch. "Lie down flat."

He scooted under the couch on his back. She climbed on top of him. There was barely enough room for the two of them.

Their faces were an inch apart.

"Come here often?" he murmured.

Her eyes flashed. "Be quiet."

Despite their circumstances, he brushed his lips over hers.

Suddenly, a light came on in the room. Footsteps sounded, and a pair of red Ferragamo shoes appeared right beside the couch.

Zane felt Monroe suck in a breath. His own pulse was hammering hard.

He heard the click of heels. "Hurry," a woman said.

The sound of a fridge opening and closing. "Got it."

"I want you, baby." The sounds of sloppy kissing. "I've never sucked a prince's cock before."

"Tonight's your lucky night, darling." There was the pop of a cork.

Monroe wrinkled her nose.

Thankfully, the amorous pair left.

"I'm not a prince, but it could be your lucky night, too," Zane said.

She elbowed him in the gut. "Let's get out of here."

***

Monroe

Vander dropped us back at the Four Seasons.

I felt pumped. Energy whizzed through my veins, leaving me jumpy.

Zane and I exited the elevator. I felt his gaze on my skin, like he was touching me.

"Wired?" he asked.

"Hell, yeah."

The doors opened into the penthouse, and I tossed my gear down.

Suddenly, he grabbed me, and yanked me against his hard body. "Watching you crack that safe—"

I rubbed against him, and felt the hard bulge against my belly. "Got you a little hot and bothered, Roth?"

He gripped me harder. "Oh, yeah."

I yanked his head down. The kiss was all tongues and teeth. *Wild.*

He nudged me back until my shoulder blades met the wall. With one hand, he pinned my wrists and flattened them against the wall above my head.

His warm breath puffed on my cheek, then he set his mouth on my neck.

"Oh, *God*." I arched for him. I was burning up.

Then his lips were back on mine, tongue plunging into my mouth.

God, Zane Roth was *so* much. A massive assault on the senses. I was ready for him just by looking at him. I'd give him anything, everything.

The thought made my belly clench. *Stop thinking, Monroe.*

Our tongues entwined. It was a hot dance, an exploration as we found out what made the other hotter.

My panties were saturated, and I felt slickness on my thighs. I also felt an empty ache that I was desperate to fill.

I yanked a hand free, and palmed the hard bulge in his pants. He groaned, sending a wicked thrill through me. I got to touch him like this, love him.

I continued stroking his cock through the fabric. His ragged moan was so sweet. I squeezed, and felt him get bigger. "Can't wait for you to slide this inside me."

"Fuck, Wildcat. Do you know how badly I want to drive it inside you? Feel you stretch as you take me?"

My womb pulsed. "Zane, I *need* you."

His gaze met mine. "I need you, too."

We pushed away from the wall, stumbling across the living area as we tore at each other's clothes.

I fumbled with his shirt, and he ripped mine over my head. Next, I attacked his belt.

"Why are you wearing so many clothes?" I complained.

He paused, and shoved my leggings down. "We can fix that."

Then I stood there, in my bra and panties. He paused, his hot gaze on me.

My legs felt weak, and I grabbed him, kissing as we moved again. Soon, my bra was also gone, and he cupped my breasts.

"You're all long, slim, but right here—" he squeezed "—perfect."

"Inside me. *Now.*"

Suddenly, he lifted me off my feet. I felt a cool surface under my butt, and realized he'd set me on the piano.

"I've never had sex on a piano," I panted.

"Me neither." He sat on the bench, and pushed my thighs apart. He gripped my panties and tore the lace off.

I moaned. "That is so hot."

"Got to taste you, wildcat." He put his tongue on me. *Oh...*

Oh, man.

He licked and teased my clit. I moaned and clamped my thighs on his head. I arched back and saw the blur of the city lights out the window.

"Zane. *Zane.*" I reared up, but he pushed me back down.

The pleasure made me buck and I let out a strangled sound. His mouth closed on my clit and sucked.

"Zane, I'm going to come. *I'm coming.*"

I heard my own husky cries. I couldn't breathe, my vision grayed. All I could do was drown in the pleasure spasming through me. His mouth was relentless. He kept licking me, like he couldn't get enough.

"No more, Zane. *Please.*" My voice was shaky. "I need you inside me."

He growled and scooped me off the piano.

"Don't make me wait," I breathed.

"I won't, Wildcat."

He set me on the dining room table by the floor-to-ceiling windows. I could practically see New York spread out beneath us.

He swiped his arm and something crashed on the floor. I gasped.

"Don't worry." He held me with one hand, the other at his zipper. I leaned forward and kissed his chest, then bit his neck. He groaned.

"Now, now," I chanted.

"Yes." He gripped his cock, nudged my legs apart, and slid inside me.

I moaned, squirming on the table.

Finally, he thrust deep, all the way inside me.

"*Zane.*" How could it feel so damn right? I hugged my thighs tight against his sides, and clenched. "Zane, *move.*"

His mouth was back on my neck, teeth raking my skin. He started thrusting—hard, deep, relentless.

"Yes!" I cried.

The table shifted beneath us, squeaking on the floor with every one of his thrusts.

I didn't care. I clung to him, panting.

"You're the hottest, sexiest thing I've ever been inside of," he grunted.

I raked my nails down his back. "You're the hottest, sexiest thing I've ever had inside me."

Our gazes met, locked. He kept up the heavy thrusts, and we didn't look away. I felt the connection right through me, like we were entwined, joined.

"*Zane*," I whispered.

I was so used to holding myself apart, protecting myself from the next blow life had for me. I'd had to deal with all my shit alone for as long as I could remember.

But right here, right now, I couldn't keep any secret or shadow from Zane.

We were pressed together, no distance between us. His thrusts picked up pace, and I clung to him, pleasure growing fast.

Then without warning, I detonated.

I screamed his name. The pleasure was so hot, and I was sure I'd pass out.

"Yes, baby, come on my cock." He hunched over me, his thrusts harder. "I'm coming inside you now, Wildcat."

"Come." I turned my head and bit his neck.

His body locked, his cock deep inside me.

"Christ, Monroe. *Fuck*." He made a sound like a roar, his body shuddering. I held him through it.

When he finally lifted his head, he took my mouth in a slow, sexy kiss.

"*Mmm*." I stroked his shoulders. They were sheened with perspiration.

We stayed locked together, holding each other. I played with the hair at the nape of his neck.

"I think I should watch you crack safes more often." His voice was low and husky.

I laughed. "Me, too."

He pulled back, and that's when I felt the slick wetness on my thighs.

Oh, shit. I stiffened.

At the look on my face, he frowned.

I licked my lips. "We, ah...forgot a condom."

"*Shit.*" He pulled me off the table to stand beside him. "Monroe, fuck. I'm sorry... I was—"

"Caught up in the inferno like me?"

"That doesn't excuse it. I should have protected you. I was tested recently and I'm clean."

"Um, I haven't been tested for ages, but it's been a *really* long, dry spell. And I've never had unprotected sex before. I think we're okay."

He brushed the hair off my face. "You on birth control?"

I nodded.

"Okay," he said.

"Okay?" I raised a brow. "Don't you want proof? You're a billionaire, Zane, you need to protect—"

"Monroe, I think I know you well enough to know you aren't trying to get pregnant and extort millions out of me." He kissed me again. Then again. "Damn, you're potent."

No one had ever thought so before. "Or you're insatiable."

He smiled and it made him look younger, sexier. "I never thought I was. It must be you."

He lifted me and I found myself tossed over his broad shoulder.

"Roth," I squealed.

He smacked my ass. "I have plans, O'Connor. For the bed, the shower, maybe the floor."

My belly quivered.

I guessed we weren't going to get much sleep.

16

I DON'T DO MOMS

Zone

Zane woke up and smiled. Monroe was plastered half over him, her face planted on his chest, and her dark hair spread over him. She had one thigh tossed over his.

The bed was wrecked again.

He stroked a hand down her back, and she made a cute, sleepy sound.

"If you want more sex, Roth," she mumbled, "You'll have to feed me first." She pressed a lazy kiss to the center of his chest.

He knew they needed to get up and touch base with Vander, but he really, really wanted to linger.

Then he heard the elevator and tensed. Shit, if Liam and Mav wanted to check in, they should've called first. They were the only people on the approved list.

Zane realized that Monroe had dozed off again.

"Zane?" a voice called.

Oh, shit. It was his mom.

Correction. There was another person on the list, he just hadn't expected her to be in New York.

He sat up, and Monroe sat as well, pushing her hair back. "What?"

"Zane, are you still in bed?" his mom called out.

Monroe's eyes went as wide as the wheels on his car. "Who is that?"

He climbed off the bed. "My mom."

"Your *mom*?" Monroe squeaked. "Why is she here? *Oh, God.*"

Monroe rolled off the bed. It was cute that she looked so panicked.

"Get dressed, Wildcat." He pulled on his jeans, and didn't bother with a shirt. He grabbed Monroe and kissed her.

"No, no, no." She pushed him away. "Don't kiss me while your mother, who birthed you, is right out there."

"Calm down."

"I don't do moms, Zane. Mine didn't hang around. Mag's didn't, either. I have no experience with them."

He kissed her nose. "Calm down and get dressed."

He strode out and left her muttering.

"Mom." His mother was standing in the living room, looking neat and tidy in a skirt and blouse. He glanced around, then winced.

His and Monroe's clothes were strewn around near the piano. Discarded shoes, his shirt hanging off the chair, Monroe's torn panties.

"This is a surprise," he said.

"I bet." Her tone was dry. She looked at his chest, then arched a brow. "I see you're busy."

He looked down. Monroe had scratched him and left two perfect gouges across his abs.

He struggled to suppress a grin. His Wildcat.

"I'll...uh..." He grabbed his wrinkled shirt off the chair and shrugged into it.

"I am sorry to interrupt you on short notice, darling. Carmen had tickets to a show and invited me. Her husband, Jeff, is sick with food poisoning. I stopped by your place...and your doorman said you were staying here."

"Yes." Zane hadn't mentioned anything to her, since he hadn't wanted her to worry. "I'm having some renovations done."

His mother's blue eyes met his. "Because someone blew up your home office?"

Shit. Zane ran his tongue over his teeth. "Mom, it's fine. My security guy is in town. You remember Vander Norcross. We're dealing with it."

One of her eyebrows rose. "That man gives me a cold shiver. He radiates this dangerous, controlled energy. Like he's waiting for a lion to charge through the door, or a tank, and he needs to stop it singlehandedly."

That was a pretty accurate description of Vander. "It makes him good at his job."

She closed the distance between them and touched Zane's face. "Are you sure you're okay?"

"I promise."

Then she glanced at the clothes. "I've intruded on your morning."

"Give me a minute and I'll pry Monroe out of the bedroom." There was every chance she'd climbed out a window, despite them being over fifty stories up.

His mother's eyes widened. "You're going to introduce me?"

He smiled. "Yes."

Her gaze roamed his face, then she smiled. "Wonderful."

"Let me get her." He marched back to the bedroom. Monroe was in his shirt and a pair of leggings, her hair loose.

Her head jerked up. "Is your mom gone?"

"No." He took Monroe's hand. "Come on, I want you to meet her."

Monroe's eyes bugged out. "What? *Noooo*. You can't introduce me to your mother."

"Yes, I can."

He towed her out. She gripped the doorjamb. "No. You've lost your mind, Roth."

Yeah, he had. Over this tough, intelligent, prickly woman. She was a survivor, and he was falling for her.

The thought didn't freak him out as much as he thought it should.

"Come on, Monroe." He tugged harder.

"You can't boss me around, Mr. Billionaire." She tugged back.

"You are the most stubborn person I know," he said. "I thought Mav took that crown, but you've stolen it."

"Actually, you're the most stubborn. And bossy, and—"

"I like her already."

Zane looked up and saw his mom staring at them, smiling.

Monroe let go of the doorjamb and slammed into his chest.

"Um... Hello," Monroe said.

"Monroe, this is my mom, Carol Roth. Mom, this is Monroe O'Connor."

His mom beamed. "It's a pleasure, Monroe."

Monroe straightened and held out a hand. His mom shook it eagerly. Monroe looked like she wanted the floor to open up and swallow her.

"It's nice to meet you, Mrs. Roth."

"Carol, please. Now, I know I interrupted, but I'd love to take you two to breakfast. I'll call down to the restaurant and organize a table."

His mother marched across to the phone on the side table. Monroe widened her eyes at Zane and jerked her head.

Yes, he was pretty sure that was code for "do something, because we aren't having breakfast with your mom" but he just shrugged, and watched heat fill her cheeks.

Not long after, he found himself seated beside Monroe and across from his mom in The Garden restaurant. Acacia trees filled the dining room, leaves brushing the ceiling. Their table was covered with various plates of breakfast delights. Monroe was doing her best to keep busy eating, so she didn't have to talk.

Zane's cell phone rang, and Vander's name flashed up on the screen. "Sorry, I need to take this." He rose.

His mom rolled her eyes. "Monroe, there's *always* some call he has to take."

Zane strode to the entry. "Vander."

"Morning. I'm on my way to you. We got something off the bug."

Zane's gut clenched. "Good. I'm just finishing up breakfast. See you soon."

He walked back to the table. Monroe's back was to him.

"Mrs. Roth, I'm not a socialite. I don't come from a great family." Monroe choked out a laugh. "That's an *understatement.* I didn't go to the right schools."

With a frown, Zane slowed down. His mom flicked him a quick glance, then refocused on Monroe.

"I mean, I went to school," Monroe said. "I own my own business."

Zane shoved his hands into his pockets. He hated hearing her talk herself down.

Monroe blew out a breath. "What I'm trying to say, is that I'm not right for your son. And by the way, you don't look old enough to have a son in his thirties."

His mother smiled. "Thank you."

"Anyway, the truth is, my younger brother is in trouble. My father's in jail. And I dragged Zane into this mess. You should tell him to run. I...don't want to see him hurt."

His gut knotted. Damn, she did a number on him. He wanted to shake her.

His mother reached across the table and took Monroe's hand.

"Monroe, I've met plenty of the society women who

went to the right schools. They'd be trying to charm me and convince me that they'd be the *perfect* Mrs. Zane Roth. You're a refreshing and honest breath of fresh air. My son is smart enough not to get dragged anywhere he doesn't want to go. And you know what I see?"

"What?" Monroe asked warily.

"A woman who clearly cares about my son."

Zane strode in and sat beside Monroe. He cupped her startled face and kissed her.

She fought him for a second, trying to break free, then she sagged against him and kissed him back. When he broke the kiss, her face was dazed.

The daze cleared. "You can't kiss me with tongue in front of your mother," she hissed.

He leaned in again—

She slapped a hand to his chest. "Keep those lips to yourself, Roth."

"We'd better finish breakfast," his mom said. "By the look on Zane's face, I assume you two have somewhere to be."

"Yes." He met Monroe's gaze. "Vander called. He's on his way over."

Monroe stiffened, then nodded.

His mother forked up some eggs. "Monroe, tell me about your business while we finish up."

"I run a locksmith shop in Hell's Kitchen. It's called Lady Locksmith."

"Oh, I've heard of it! All female locksmiths. A friend of mine is involved with Nightingale House."

Monroe nodded. "I donate my time there."

"She said your locksmiths are amazing."

Monroe smiled. "Thank you. I have a great team."

Zane leaned back in his chair, and smiled as well.

Monroe

I kept my smile up as Mrs. Roth left.

Zane waved.

Once Carol Roth was out of sight, I slapped his chest. Then I swiveled and strode toward the penthouse elevator. I cut through the lobby like a shark on the hunt.

Zane caught up with me. "Monroe—"

"You should never have introduced me to your mother."

He touched the button for the elevator. "I disagree."

"I'm a *thief*. The daughter of a thief. My brother is in debt to the Russian mafia. If your mother knew the full story—"

The doors opened and he pushed me inside, then swiped his card. "My mother didn't grow up wealthy, Monroe. She worked two jobs to support me. She had a deadbeat husband who abandoned her for a younger woman. She admires your business, and she trusts my judgment." He backed me into the wall.

"I'm not sure I trust your judgment," I muttered.

He nipped my lips. "I guess I need to convince you."

The kiss was getting heated as the doors opened.

Vander was waiting for us, and looked mildly amused. Or at least, I thought he did. He was a hard man to read—his rugged face stayed very impassive.

"Hey." Zane lifted his chin at the man.

We settled on the couches and Vander set his phone down on the coffee table. "The bug picked this up this morning."

Franz's German-accented voice came through the speaker. "She was *very* energetic, and her friend was, as well."

A chorus of male laughter.

"These guys are assholes," I said.

"No disagreement from me," Zane replied.

"When do we move our shiny, new sparkler?" Another voice. It sounded like Alamanni.

"The buyer is arriving in a few days," Franz said.

I leaned forward, my pulse spiking.

"I want to see it again," someone said. That would be Bissette.

"No," Franz replied.

"But Franz—"

"It's in the safe. Protected."

What safe, assholes? I met Zane's gaze.

"That big, old safe is a fortress," Alamanni noted.

I frowned. *What safe were they talking about?*

"I just wish it wasn't in the basement. It's creepy down there." Bissette made a sound.

Vander ended the recording.

"A safe in the basement?" I said.

Vander nodded. "The house has a basement with a wine cellar. I did some more digging, and found a reference to an old Diebold safe being in the house many years ago. The safe was made in 1877."

I sat back and whistled. "Old school. Diebold

started making bank vaults and safes in the mid-1800s. They were big, sturdy, and secure. They became famous after the Great Fire of Chicago in 1871, because their safes survived. Everything stored in them was undamaged. Some of the antique safes are truly beautiful."

"It appears that this one is called a Model 5D," Vander added.

I froze. "No way."

Vander's brows drew together. "That's what Ace said."

I shook my head. "5Ds were really rare, and built tough. It would be hard to crack."

Zane took her hand. "Really?"

I nodded. "I know one person who's done it."

"Who?"

I sighed, my belly in knots. "My dad." I shook my head. "He has some old notes. I'll pull everything up that I have on the Diebold 5D."

"We can't go in tonight—"

My head jerked up. "What? Why? I want my brother safe and this over with, Vander, I—"

The security expert shook his head. "Franz and his buddies are hosting a big party at their place tonight. There will be security and lots of guests."

Zane squeezed my arm. "Maguire's fine for now. I know it's hard to wait, but I suspect you need time to research the Diebold, and Vander needs to plan our way in."

I sank back against the cushions. "Okay."

"We'll go in tomorrow night," Vander said. "The

three of them will be at another party at Club Real. We'll have a clear shot at the safe."

Blowing out a breath, I nodded. "Tomorrow night. I need to make a call. Get my manager to take care of the store for the next couple of days."

"I need to call my assistant, too," Zane said. "And give him a heart attack by asking him to cancel all my meetings for today and tomorrow."

More he was sacrificing for me. I just stared at him.

He ran a finger down my nose.

I couldn't bring myself to call Sabrina. She'd try to interrogate me. I dashed off a text to tell her I was sorting something out with Maguire, and could she take care of the store.

Then I got to work. Zane found a sleek, little laptop for me, and I sat at the dining room table. I started researching the 5D safe. I got onto my cloud storage and pulled up my scans of my father's old notes. I should have destroyed them, but I'd never been able to do it. His old journals were in a box at my apartment, and one weekend, I'd scanned them all.

A mug of coffee appeared beside me, and I blinked. Zane's handsome face came into view.

"Hey," he smiled.

I rubbed my eyes, then sipped the coffee, and groaned. "Thanks."

"You've been at it for hours."

"I have?"

He kissed me. This kiss was slow and deep. He took his time. *Yum.* All our previous encounters had been fast, hot, and furious.

This was different.

"Quit distracting me," I whispered.

"I can't help it. You're cute when you're concentrating."

I wrinkled my nose.

"By the way, the work at my penthouse is done," he told her.

"Already?"

"I pay well."

"I bet," I said dryly.

"And I have a friend in construction. We'll head back there this evening. And after this, when Maguire is safe, I'm locking you and I in there for several days. I'll even get a few bottles of good Irish whiskey."

My lips twitched. "Don't you work?"

"I'm the boss. I can take time off." His gaze turned thoughtful. "Honestly, I can't remember the last time I took more than a day or so." He squeezed my hand. "But I want to spend time with you. Without the explosions, jewel thieves, and the mafia."

My heart squeezed. "Sounds great."

The whirr of the elevator made both of us glance over.

Zane scowled. "I need to tell the concierge to stop letting people up."

Two men stepped out—Liam and Maverick.

Uh-oh. Neither looked happy.

"We hadn't heard from you," Mav said darkly.

"You missed training with Simeon today," Liam said.

Mav crossed his arms over his chest. "You haven't returned our calls."

Liam looked at me, a faint smile on his face, but a cool, assessing look in his eyes. "And now I see why."

Zane rose and I did too. Something told me I was at a huge disadvantage if I stayed sitting.

Mav Rivera looked like he was on the warpath. I wanted to run, anything, to escape the scrutiny. They looked pissed, and they had a right to be. I'd landed their friend in trouble.

"I'll just—" I took a step away.

Zane dragged me back and clamped me to his side. "You're not going anywhere, Monroe."

Mav cocked his head. "So, you know her name is Monroe O'Connor. She's the daughter of Terry O'Connor, who's an incarcerated thief."

I flinched.

"Yes, I know that," Zane said.

"And she's in the family business."

"Mav, I know who Monroe is."

"And yet she's here, and you're clearly fucking her, and she's landed you in fucking hot water."

I jerked, but Zane held me tighter.

"Cool it, Mav. The necklace was targeted by jewel thieves—"

"Yes, *her*." Maverick shot me a look that made my insides shrivel.

"You're right," I said. "I keep telling him to get away from me, but the man doesn't listen."

"Quiet," Zane said.

I turned. "It's safer for you. I want you safe, Zane."

Something moved through his eyes. "Monroe—"

"I don't want anyone to hurt you. When the bomb

went off—" My voice cracked, and I cleared my throat. "You should walk away."

"*Fuck* that." He kissed me.

With his lips on mine, I kind of forgot about the two cranky billionaires in the room. I kissed him back, sliding my arm around his neck.

There was a clearing throat, and one amused chuckle.

I blinked and saw Liam smiling at me. Mav wasn't smiling, but he was eyeing me with contemplation on his rugged face.

"Sit," Zane told his friends. "I'll get you coffee, but if you're rude to her, I'll punch you."

Liam sat, crossing his legs and resting one ankle on his knee. "I like my face just the way it is."

"Pretty boy." Mav sat with a grunt and crossed his arms over his chest. "I could take you, Roth." Then he looked at the laptop and the safe schematics on it, and raised a brow. "Planning another robbery?"

I met his dark gaze. "Yes."

Liam smiled again. "You're even more attractive as a brunette than a blonde."

"I'm already sleeping with a billionaire." The thought still made me a little queasy. "I don't need another one."

Zane strode back in and set the mugs down by his friends, then he pressed a hand to the back of my neck and sat.

"Monroe's brother is being held by local Russian mafia."

"Bloody hell," Liam murmured.

"They asked her to get the necklace in return for his life."

I felt Liam and Mav looking at me, but kept my gaze on my lap. I didn't care what they thought of me. Okay, I did—they were Zane's best friends—but regardless of what they thought, I had to save my brother.

"Unfortunately, some opportunistic jewel thieves entered the picture, and bombed my place and took the necklace. We know who they are and we're stealing it back."

"Fuck," Mav muttered and looked at the laptop. "And it's in an old Diebold?"

Zane nodded.

"They're hard to crack."

"I can do it," I said. *Hopefully.*

Maverick's dark eyes studied me. "You really cracked my Riv3000?"

I nodded.

"I want to hire you as a consultant. Show me how you did it, and help me design it better."

I smiled. "Lady Locksmith would love to do business with Rivera Tech. By the way, we're very expensive."

Liam hid his laugh in his coffee.

"Oh, and a friend of mine hacked your system to get the safe schematics."

Mav's face went a little red. "I'd like to hire him too."

I wrinkled my nose. "I'll talk to him, but he's not really a team player."

Zane looked at his friends. "This will all be over tomorrow night, once we get the necklace back and Monroe's brother is safe."

Again, I felt a wave of queasiness at the thought of Zane breaking the law to help me. I glanced at his friends and an idea formed. I faced Mav and Liam. "There is no reason for him to come with me tomorrow night. Talk some sense into him."

Zane growled. "Monroe—"

Liam shrugged. "He's always had this annoying quirk of doing whatever the hell he wants."

I looked to Mav. His face was impassive and he just lifted one broad shoulder. No help there.

I rolled my eyes, and Zane pressed a finger under my chin and tipped my face up. His lips brushed mine. "It's going to be all right."

Deep inside, I really, really hoped that was true.

17

IT'S JUST A COFFEE

Zane

When Zane woke, the first thing he registered was that he was back in his own bed in his own place.

The second thing was that he was alone.

Worry hit him. Had Monroe left?

Then he heard music drifting in from somewhere. He breathed deep and smelled Monroe on the pillows.

Funny how he'd preferred sleeping alone all his adult life, yet now he missed having her sleek body wrapped around him.

He knew she was worried—about him, about Mag, about how to crack the Diebold safe.

It would all be over tonight.

All Zane cared about was keeping her safe.

He headed to the bathroom and pulled on some long, black pajama pants. As he headed toward the kitchen, he was assaulted by scents and sounds.

Rock music was pumping from somewhere, accompanied by Monroe's enthusiastic but off-key singing. The scent was something delicious baking.

He rounded the corner and stopped. She was at the island, wearing only one of his white business shirts, her raven hair in a messy bun on top of her head. She held a wooden spoon like a microphone and was dancing. She also had a streak of flour on one cheek.

His gut clenched into a hard ball. She somehow looked ridiculous and gorgeous at the same time, and he knew without a doubt, that she was his.

Simeon was right.

Zane would grow old with this woman. She'd hopefully have his babies, make him laugh or growl, and keep him on his toes.

And he knew if he told her that, she'd run, as fast as her long legs could carry her.

Her head jerked up and she spotted him. She grinned, then touched the portable speaker sitting on the island.

"Sorry, did I wake you?"

"No. I woke because you weren't there." He moved over to her and touched his mouth to hers. She pressed her hands to his chest, dusting flour on his pecs.

"Sorry." Her lips twitched.

He reached down and pinched her butt. "You don't look sorry. What are you doing?"

"Stress baking." She nudged a strand of hair off her cheek with the back of her hand. "When I'm stressed, I bake."

He scanned the ingredients spread on the island, and

the dough resting in the bowl. "I didn't even know I had stuff to bake with."

She smiled. "I'm making my world-famous salted butter oatmeal choc-chip cookies."

Zane stilled. "For me?"

She nodded.

Suddenly his throat felt tight. "World-famous, huh?"

"Yep. My secret is the salted butter, and I don't use eggs, just a little oil."

He leaned against the island, watching her competently roll small balls of dough in her hand and place them on a tray. She flattened them with the press of her palm.

"Where did you learn to bake?"

"A neighbor, when I was about ten. Her name was Mrs. Varley. Sometimes, Da would take off on a job, and leave me and Mag alone."

Zane blinked. "He left his young children? Alone?"

She touched his cheek. "Hey, it was over a long time ago. We survived. Mrs. Varley would check in with us, and she taught me to bake." Monroe smiled. "She always smelled like cookies."

He could easily picture a dark-haired little girl, responsible beyond her years, and hungry for someone to look out for her.

"Well, here's to Mrs. Varley," he said.

There was a ding from the fancy oven he never used. Monroe swiveled, and his gaze dropped to her bare legs.

Hmm.

She pulled out a tray holding a cake and set it on some sort of rack.

"What's that?" he asked.

She rolled her eyes. "A hockey puck."

"Funny." He moved closer. It smelled damn good.

"It's the cake I made for you."

Warmth filled his chest. "I get a cake too?"

"I figured since you're a billionaire, there's nothing I can get you that you can't get yourself. I wanted to say thank you, for everything you've done for me."

"Monroe..." He tucked that still-lose strand of hair back behind her ear.

She smiled. "I couldn't buy you something, so I figured I'd make you something."

"Thank you," he murmured.

"It's red velvet."

His body locked. "That's my favorite."

"I know."

He spun her to face him. Apart from his mom, no one had ever gone out of their way to find out what his favorite cake was. "How did you know?"

"I not-so-subtly asked your mom yesterday." She grabbed the wooden spoon again.

The mom she'd tried to avoid talking to. *Damn.* Emotion ran through him.

Her brow creased. "Zane?"

He kissed her.

She moaned, the wooden spoon clattered to the floor, and her hands gripped his biceps.

He slid his arms around her and boosted her onto the counter.

"Oh," she breathed.

"I love red velvet, but I want a taste of you now." He

pushed her back on the marble, and bunched the shirt up, uncovering that sweet body he couldn't get enough of.

He put his mouth on her, over her plain black panties.

Monroe cried out, her hands tangling in his hair.

Need riding him, Zane pushed the gusset aside, and pushed his tongue inside her.

She made a strangled cry. "*Zane.*"

He licked at her, pulling in her honeyed taste. "That, that right there. You screaming my name is the best gift you could give me. Now lie back, and take what I give you."

Gray eyes met his. "Whatever you give me, I'll take."

Monroe

I finished dressing after my shower, sliding into my dark jeans and favorite red sweater. My legs still felt like limp noodles. Zane had gone down on me in the kitchen, then fucked me on the island until I was hoarse from screaming. I ran my tongue over my teeth. My belly was still jittering.

I headed out. He was standing at the island, looking at something on a tablet, and eating a slice of the red velvet cake.

He looked up and smiled.

My legs felt even weaker. I'd bake him a cake every day if it earned me that smile.

Mentally, I shook my head. *Do not get too attached to the hot, sexy billionaire, Monroe.*

No one hung around long in my life, except Mag.

"Let's go down to the coffee shop downstairs," Zane said. "I need a mocha with an extra shot."

"Sure." I could do with the caramel latte.

In the elevator, he slung an arm across my shoulders.

"How are you feeling about the Diebold?" he asked.

"Honestly, I'm terrified. I'm not a hundred percent sure I can crack it. I like to take time to plan, and to practice." I huffed out a breath. "The longer we're in that house, the higher the risk that we'll get caught. Mag is depending on me."

It all felt like a heavy weight settling on my shoulders.

Zane ran a hand down my ponytail. "It's going to be all right."

I nodded, but all my hot-sex-in-the-kitchen vibes were gone. "I want to spend most of today going over the notes on the Diebold again. I *have* to get it right."

He tugged my ponytail. "Let's get you some coffee."

The coffee shop next to Zane's building was busy. When he took my hand, I jolted and tried to tug free.

He tightened his hold.

"People might see us," I hissed.

"So?" He looked totally-unconcerned. "I'm not a rock star or an actor. Paparazzi don't follow me around. They usually snap pictures at parties and events."

I glanced out the plate-glass windows of the cozy coffee shop, searching for anyone with a camera.

Shaking his head, he tugged me into the line. "Relax."

"Oh, wow, you're Zane Roth," a voice said.

We turned our heads. A bunch of young people—college students in their late teens or early twenties—sat around on some of the armchairs. They all had AirPods in their ears, phones in their hands, and backpacks on the floor by their feet.

"I'm majoring in finance," one young man said, awe on his face. "I want to *be* you when I grow up."

"Well, study hard, and work harder," Zane said.

"Can we get a photo?" another young man asked.

Zane glanced at me, a rueful look on his face.

"Go." I shooed him.

While he was busy, I ordered the coffees and paid. I watched Zane smile and talk with the kids.

He might not be a rock star, but those kids were looking at him like he was one.

"Monroe," the barista called out.

I nodded and grabbed the coffee cups. The sweet scent of coffee hit me. I really needed this today.

When I turned, Zane was heading my way.

"Sorry," he said.

"No problem." I held out his coffee.

He took it slowly, a funny look on his face. It was similar to the one he had when I pulled the red velvet cake out of the oven.

"Zane?"

He looked up, his hazel eyes alive with something that made my throat tight.

"I just realized that no woman has ever bought me a coffee before."

I dragged in a breath. Jeez, who were these women he'd been mixing with? "It's just a coffee, Zane."

"No. It's not." He tugged me to him, careful not to spill our coffees. Then he kissed me.

I forgot where we were. The coffee shop melted away and I kissed him back, lost in him.

Then I heard chuckles, followed by a whistle.

We broke apart and I glanced over. The college kids were smiling at us, but I noted that one was holding up her phone, taking a snap.

"Shit." Zane shielded me and we hurried out. He towed me back into his building and into the elevator.

He backed me against the wall, and kissed me again. His kiss held an edge. He bit my bottom lip, and I moaned.

"You going to fuck me on the kitchen counter again?" I asked breathlessly.

"I'm thinking about bending you over the couch this time."

My belly spasmed.

The doors opened and we stumbled inside the penthouse.

Zane took my coffee and set them both down on a side table. Then his hands were in my hair, tugging the tie free.

"I can't get enough of you, Monroe."

"*Zane*." I bit his lip this time and listened to a growl rumble through him.

He lifted his head. "What do you see when you look at me?"

I frowned, uncertain of where he was going with this. "Zane, I see you." *What else would I see?*

His lips curved into a smile. "Everyone else in my

life, apart from my mom, Liam, and Mav, see a billionaire, a businessman, a bank account. But you see me, and I see you, Monroe."

My heart clenched. "Zane—"

"I see *you*."

Then he was kissing me again, and all I could think about was him.

Zane's cell phone rang.

"Shit," he muttered. "Ignore it."

It stopped ringing, and his tongue plunged into my mouth. I yanked him closer, pulling his shirt up.

His phone started ringing again and he cursed.

"You'd better check it," I said.

He yanked it out of his pocket and stiffened. "It's Vander." He pressed the button. "Vander, hi. You're on speaker with me and Monroe."

"We've got a problem."

Vander's hard words made my stomach clench.

"Franz, Alamanni, and Bissette's plans got canceled. They aren't going out to Club Real. They're staying in tonight."

"No." I shook my head. This was a disaster.

"There's more," Vander said. "Tomorrow, the necklace will be gone. The buyer is arriving in the morning."

I pressed a fist to my chest. *No, no, no.*

"We still have to go in tonight," Vander said.

Go in with the three assholes, and who knew who else, in the house. I bit my lip.

"I assume you have a backup plan?" Zane asked.

"Yeah," Vander said. "I know Franz approached you for a business deal."

Zane frowned. "I assumed that was bogus. Just a way to scope out my penthouse."

"It's not bogus. Prince Franz has been shopping around for investors for his new gin."

Zane nodded thoughtfully. "I suddenly feel interested in investing in alcoholic beverages."

With a gasp, I gripped his shirt. "No! They blew up your place. You can't just walk in there."

"They don't know that I know it was them."

"Arrange a meet," Vander said. "You go in, and take Monroe as your assistant. She excuses herself to use the restroom, and gets to the safe. Monroe, you'll have to be fast."

I felt sick. I wasn't sure I could crack the Diebold, let alone do it fast. I'd be risking both Zane and my brother. The brother I loved, despite his screwups, and the man I cared for more than I should.

I'd do anything to keep them safe.

My queasy stomach turned over. Yes, I'd do anything to keep them safe. Even talk to the one person I hadn't spoken with in years.

"I need to talk with my dad."

18

HEARTS CRACK FAR EASIER THAN SAFES

Monroe

I emailed my father through a service that printed emails out and had them delivered to prisoners at mail call.

I wasn't sure that he'd even get the message to call me in time, so two hours later, when I saw the area code for the prison on my phone, I felt a churn of emotion in my belly.

Zane gave me some privacy to talk with my father. He was also waiting for his scheduled call with Prince Franz.

My stomach turned in circles. I didn't want to do this, but I also didn't want Zane in danger. And I wanted Mag safe. I blinked back tears. I knew life rarely gave you what you wanted. You had to power on through.

I thumbed the phone and the call connected.

"Will you accept a call from Terry O'Connor?" a voice asked.

"Yes." I waited for my dad to come on the line.

"'Lo."

My father had been born and raised in America, but still had a faint trace of Ireland in his voice.

"Hi, Da."

There was a pause. "Monroe. It's been a long time."

"Yeah, I know." I turned to look out the windows, but I couldn't focus on the view. "Da, Maguire is in trouble."

"That boy has a wild streak in him. I did, too, at the same age."

"He got himself in debt. To the Russian mafia."

My father cursed.

"They're going to kill him, unless I steal something for them."

"Jaysus."

My father's voice brought up a confusing mix of emotions. It was strange to both love and hate someone.

"I need to crack a Diebold 5D."

My father whistled. "Old school. Tough."

"I know. And I know you did it once."

"Yeah." There was a fond note in his voice. "It wasn't easy."

"I need to know how, Da. For Mag."

My father blew out a breath. "You know it ain't as easy as A to B and B to C, Monroe."

"I know." A strong memory of sitting at my father's knee as he taught me how to finesse a safe hit me. "I... won't have much time. Other people are risking their lives to help me."

"A man?"

My hand tightened on the phone. "Yes."

"Don't let your heart get involved, Mon. Hearts crack far easier than safes."

I knew that. Mine was patched up and scarred from my childhood. Although I suspected Zane Roth could shatter it beyond repair.

"I'll tell you what I can," my father said.

As he spoke, I took notes. "Thanks, Da."

"Remember, I taught you that each safe is different. Even if they're the same model, and made by the same people, each one has quirks that makes them unique. You have to respect that. You have to use that."

I dragged in a breath. "I will." I saw Zane step out of the bedroom, his face serious. "I've got to go."

"Monroe, be careful."

"I will. Bye, Da."

"Okay?" Zane wandered over.

"No." Talking with my father always left me churned up. Remembering the tough times, the rare, good times, and feeling that sense of loss for what I'd never had. I'd never, ever be a normal woman, who'd grown up with a great family that included loving parents.

Zane hugged me. "This will all be over soon."

But would we all come out in one piece?

"Vander's coming over. He wants to go over the plan again."

"You called Franz?" I asked.

Zane nodded. "We're meeting him at six o'clock this evening."

My heart leaped into my throat. That was only a few hours away.

Vander arrived, holding two vests. "Latest in bulletproof tech. Lightweight and not bulky. You can hide them under your clothes. They're barely be noticeable."

"Bulletproof vests?" I swallowed. "Why?"

"They have a bodyguard. Former French military. He's armed, so I'm not taking any chances."

I nodded, feeling sick.

"Monroe, I arranged for some clothes for you to wear," Zane said. "They're in the bedroom."

Time to get ready. Fighting my nerves, I headed for the bedroom. I stripped off my jeans and looked at myself in the mirror.

Make this work, Monroe. Crack the safe. Get Zane out safely. Save your brother.

Piece of cake. I barely stopped a hysterical giggle.

My phone beeped and I saw several missed calls from Sabrina. I sent a quick text to my friend. There was only one thing that would keep Sabrina off my back.

There's a guy. I'll tell you soon.

Ooh! Invite him to the wedding. I want details!!!

I pulled the vest on. It hugged my torso like a corset. Then I dressed in the clothes Zane had left out.

Oh, God. I pulled my hair up in a twist, and slipped on the glasses Zane had included. Last, I slipped into a pair of heels.

I usually avoided heels, but I'd worn more of them this week than the last few months combined. These were nice, though. They were black, with sexy red soles.

I walked out. "Do you have a sexy-librarian fetish, Roth?"

When I saw him, my mouth went dry.

He was in a dark-blue suit, with a white shirt and blue tie. He was so damn handsome.

His eyes lit up. "I didn't before, but I might now."

His gaze roamed over me. I wore a long, tight, black skirt, with a pinstriped shirt tucked in over the vest. My hair was up, and the glasses were perched on my nose.

He walked over and touched my temple. "You look good enough to fuck on my desk."

I felt a surge of heat between my thighs. "You need a minute to take it all in?"

"Yeah." He adjusted himself discreetly.

The small moment made me smile, but it didn't take long before it dissolved. "I'm scared. For you, for Mag."

"But not for yourself." He smoothed some hair back behind my ear. "It's going to be okay, Monroe."

He touched his hand to my cheek, and I pressed into his strong palm. Leaning on him felt so good. I'd miss it when he was finally gone from my life.

Vander appeared. "Time to go. I'll act as your driver. I can't come in, since they might recognize me, but I'll be right outside and listening." He held out a hand. On his palm was a set of earrings and a pair of cufflinks.

"Put these on. They have listening devices embedded in them."

I took the pretty silver studs and slipped them in my ears. I watched Zane expertly slide the cufflinks into his shirt sleeves.

"Ms. O'Connor, your gear." Zane handed me a brief-case. "Your tools are hidden under the tablet and papers."

I stiffened my spine and nodded. "Let's do this."

Zane

Zane walked up the steps to the house on the Upper East Side.

"It's easier coming in the front door," he murmured.

Beside him, Monroe made a sound. She was tense, lines of stress around her mouth.

"Hey, relax. We don't want to tip them off."

She nodded and straightened her shoulders.

"I really want to kiss you," he said.

"After this, you can kiss me as much as you want."

"I know a good deal when I hear one." Zane lifted his fist and knocked. "Let's get this over and done with

The door was opened by a guard. The man eyed Zane, then Monroe.

"Zane Roth to see Prince Franz," Zane said.

The guard nodded and opened the door. The man didn't pat them down, or check Monroe's briefcase. *Thank God.*

They were led into a spacious living area.

"Ah, Mr. Roth, pleasure." Franz flowed forward. He was wearing tight trousers, and a shirt in an eye-watering yellow. "I'm glad you changed your mind about talking business with me."

"I was intrigued." Zane shook the man's hand.

"You're lucky. We'll be leaving New York tomorrow."

"I'm glad you could fit me in. This is my assistant, Ms. O'Connor."

Franz's eyes moved over her, his lips curving. Zane wanted to punch him.

"Truly a pleasure, Ms. O'Connor."

She kept an impassive face and nodded.

"Come." The man waved them in. "Would you like a drink? You should try my gin, Zane. May I call you Zane?"

"Sure," Zane replied.

Zane sat on the couch and Monroe sat beside him. Franz made small talk as he made the drinks.

Bissette and Alamanni wandered in, two women with them. It looked like they'd all been drinking for a while.

"Ah, Zane, let me introduce my associates, Jean-Baptiste and Leo."

Introductions were made. The newcomers sat on chairs in the corner, pouring themselves more drinks.

"Let's talk business, Your Highness," Zane said.

"Excuse me." Monroe rose. "May I use your restroom?"

The prince waved a hand, and the guard jerked his head toward a doorway.

Monroe caught Zane's gaze, then took her briefcase and walked out.

Do your thing, Wildcat.

Franz's face moved into serious lines. "I heard you recently had some unpleasantness at your home, Zane."

"Yes. Thieves."

"I'm sorry to hear that." Franz actually looked sympathetic.

"They stole a valuable necklace."

Franz made a noncommittal noise. "Terrible, terrible."

"My insurance is dealing with it. So, tell me about your gin?"

Franz handed a heavy, cut-crystal glass over, and launched into his grand plans to make Prince Gin the number one gin in the world.

Zane took a tiny sip. Had Monroe made it downstairs? Was she working on the safe? "I'll need my team to run numbers."

The prince waved a hand. "Numbers are boring to me."

Zane smiled. "But not when there's a dollar sign in front of them."

Franz laughed uproariously. "That is true."

"I think you have an interesting product." Zane sipped again and held the glass up. Bland, uninspired, and boring. "And with your image to promote it, it's sure to be a winner."

Franz's chest puffed up. "Thank you." He looked to the door. "Where is your lovely assistant?" He leaned forward. "*That ass.* You must tap it as much as you can." The man winked.

Zane kept his anger in check. "Ms. O'Connor is my employee."

Franz's face sharpened. "So, she's available?"

Zane leaned forward as well. "No."

The prince leaned back and waved a finger. "Sly, I like that."

How could these assholes have broken into his place? They didn't seem to have the smarts.

They continued to sip the gin, and Franz talked about stocking clubs and bars across Europe. He also wanted help to break into the US market.

"That actor, he does well marketing his gin." Franz threw an arm out. "But I can do better. I'm a prince."

"Hmm. I'm sure we can put together a stellar marketing plan."

Franz frowned. "The sexy Ms. O'Connor has been gone a while."

At the door, the bodyguard stiffened.

Shit. "She did say that she was feeling a little off. So, Franz, what about a sponsorship with some luxury brands? Maybe yachts or cars?" *Come on, Monroe.*

"I love yachts and cars. Did I tell you that I race?"

"Really?"

The bodyguard slipped out and a trickle of sweat slid down Zane's spine. A moment later the bodyguard returned. "The woman isn't in the bathroom."

Fuck. Zane tensed.

Franz rose, frowning. "Find her."

Zane stirred. "Your Highness, we still have things to discuss."

Bissette and Alamanni had lost interest in the women. They were clearly picking up on the undercurrent of tension.

"Babe, get your friend and go upstairs," Alamanni said. "We'll be up soon for a private party."

The women left with sulky looks and the click of heels. They both shot Zane hungry looks.

Franz turned, swirling the last of his gin in his glass.

"Why did you change your mind about meeting me, Roth?"

Zane shrugged, staying relaxed, even though his pulse spiked. "I always take my time to assess all business opportunities—"

The bodyguard charged back in. "The door to the basement is unlocked."

Franz cursed and looked at Zane. He set the glass down with a click. "You know it was us who stole the necklace."

Bissette and Alamanni leaped up.

The prince gestured at the bodyguard. The man pulled a gun and aimed it at Zane.

Shit. "Settle down. There's no need for guns." *Please be listening, Vander.* "I'm sure we can come to an—"

"Let's find the woman," Franz barked.

The bodyguard moved behind Zane, pressing the gun into his lower back.

Ah, hell. He followed the assholes out of the room, and down the stairs to the basement. They rounded a corner, and he saw Monroe crouched in front of a large, old-fashioned safe. Her briefcase was sitting open beside her, a small drill resting next to it.

The door to the safe was open, and the Phillips-Morley necklace was in her hand.

"Ah, Ms. O'Connor has more talents than just looking fuckable," Franz drawled.

Monroe stood and swiveled. The light gleamed off the sapphire in the necklace. She looked at Zane, her face white.

Zane breathed deeply. Vander would come to their

rescue. They just needed to stay calm. "Franz, we can work out a deal—"

"*No!* You tried to steal from me." The prince reached forward and snatched the necklace from Monroe's hand.

"You stole from him first," she snapped.

"But someone else is pulling your strings," Zane said. "You aren't smart enough to have planned all of this."

Franz's face twisted. "I'm smarter than you, Roth. I'm not the one with the gun pointed at me."

Monroe made a sound and Zane saw fear on her face.

"I assume you're part of the Black Fox gang," Zane said. "They give you orders."

The prince jerked.

Zane felt little satisfaction about being right. "The Black Foxes are going down. You must know what happened in San Francisco." Vander's team had helped bring down the leader of the international gang of thieves. "The police and Interpol are pulling apart the gang as we speak. Your days are numbered."

Franz tossed his head back. "There's nothing linking us to the gang."

"Our conversation is being recorded," Zane said. "I'm not sure you'll like jail. No yachts, supercars, gin, or women."

"No." Franz started sweating, and the other men shifted uneasily.

"We have to do something," Alamanni said sharply.

Fuck. They were panicking. Zane lifted his hands higher. "Let's talk calmly—"

"Shut up!" Franz yelled.

Shit. Zane needed to get Monroe out of here. "Just listen—"

"I said, shut *up*." Franz snatched the gun off the bodyguard. "I'll kill you both."

Zane's stomach knotted. *Where the hell was Vander?* "Franz—"

The man swiveled to Monroe, then back to Zane.

"Calm down," Monroe said.

No, Zane didn't want the man focused on her. "Franz, look at me. We'll deal with this like businessmen."

The younger man's hands were shaking. "Quiet." He lifted the gun, his finger trembling on the trigger. "This is all your fault, Roth."

"No!" Monroe leaped in front of Zane.

The gun went off.

No. *No.* Zane's heart felt like it burst through his chest.

He saw Monroe's body jerk.

No.

He caught her and sank to the floor.

19

I HATE STITCHES

Monroe

God, it hurt. *A lot.*

I tried to breathe. It felt like I had a rock on my chest. I wheezed.

"Monroe. *Fuck.*" Zane cradled me. His face twisted with worry. "Take it easy." He patted me down gently. "Breathe slowly."

The pain was slowly subsiding. This had to be what a battering ram to the chest felt like.

"Look at me," he said.

I stared into his beautiful, hazel eyes.

"I've got you, Wildcat."

The pain receded to manageable levels. Now, I was aware of Franz and the others arguing.

"We can't kill Zane Roth," one of the men said.

Oh, no. This was bad. Really bad.

"I've already shot the woman. We're in too deep." Franz paced jerkily, gun in hand. He was losing it.

The bodyguard looked nervous.

"We can come to an agreement," Zane said quietly.

All gazes swung to us and I stayed still.

"I have a lot of money," Zane said. "I'll pay you all to leave. Leave us and the necklace, and go."

The men fell silent.

My pulse rocketed. They were thinking about it.

Then Franz shook his head. "No. He'll tell the authorities."

"Look, I just want to get Monroe out of here—"

"You should never have tried to steal from me!" Franz screamed.

"Oh, that's rich," I bit out. "You stole it first. You think you're special. 'Ooh, I'm a prince.'" I mimicked his accent badly. "You're trash. You're a bad person. Who your family is does not make you—" I met Zane's gaze "—good, bad, or special. It's who you make yourself. It's your deeds and actions that count, and Franz, you suck."

The man spluttered. "I am a prince!"

"No one cares," I said.

"God, I'm totally falling in love with you," Zane said.

I jerked. "What?" No, he couldn't mean that.

His fingers stroked my cheek. "Let's get out of here first."

"Why isn't she bleeding?" Alamanni said.

"She's wearing a vest," the bodyguard said.

Zane pulled me up. I glanced to the door. *Come on, Vander.*

"Just walk away," Zane said.

"We need the money," Bissette said.

"So, you go out and get a job," I said. "Work, and be productive."

"Work?" Franz said. "But I'm a prince."

"Still with that?" I shook my head. "It doesn't make you special. From everything I've seen, you're an entitled asshole."

With a roar, Franz charged.

Oh, no.

Zane shoved me out of the way.

The men collided. The gun flew through the air, and hit the floor.

Then Zane turned into a total badass.

My mouth dropped open. I watched him punch Franz, and follow through with a fancy kick to the man's gut. Franz doubled over.

Zane whirled, and followed with more hits and kicks.

He clearly did some sort of martial arts.

Franz staggered and went down on one knee. Then he pulled something from his pocket.

"Zane, he has a knife!" I screamed.

My pulse went crazy.

Franz slashed at Zane, swinging wildly. Zane dodged, dancing backward.

Fear turned my stomach into a tight ball.

All of a sudden, Franz swiveled and changed direction. He ran straight at me.

Oh, shit.

I threw myself to the side.

"Monroe!" Zane shouted.

A hand grabbed the back of my shirt and spun me around.

Franz yanked me back against his chest, and I felt the prick of something sharp at my throat.

Oh, God. *God.* I froze.

Franz pressed the knife to my skin, just below my jaw line. He was breathing heavily.

"Take it easy, Franz," Zane said.

"Don't come any closer!" the prince screamed.

Zane held his hands up. I tried to breathe through my panic.

"Just let her go," Zane said. "You don't want to do this."

"Franz—" Bissette said.

"Shut up! All of you." Franz shook his head. "I just wanted to make some money. Have some fun."

My anger swelled, growing like a tsunami. This was my life. Zane's life. Franz thought he could do whatever he wanted, take whatever he wanted, use whomever he wanted.

Fuck that.

"You entitled piece of shit." I elbowed him. Hard. I rammed him again in the gut. He grunted. I shifted and elbowed him in the jaw.

His head snapped back. I turned and slammed my palm into his face.

Something cracked under my hand, and blood flowed down over his mouth and chin. He howled and his hold on me loosened.

I tore free and punched him in the stomach. "How's that feel?"

I saw Zane advancing.

"Is this fun?" I hit Franz again.

The man's eyes sparked. "Bitch!"

He rammed into me—then jammed his knife into my side.

There was a sharp, burning sting. *Shit.*

He'd found the gap at the side of my vest.

"Monroe!" Zane reached me and slammed his fist into Franz's face.

The man collapsed with a groan. The necklace fell from his pocket and hit the floor.

Then my legs dissolved, and I was falling.

But Zane caught me.

"Monroe... *Shit.*" He pressed his hand to my side.

I saw the blood on my shirt. *Oh, God.* "Wow, shot and stabbed in one day." Dizziness swamped me.

"Quiet." Zane tore my shirt off, leaving me in my vest. He wadded the shirt against my side. "Just lie still."

"Okay." I didn't think I could move if I wanted to.

His gaze met mine. He looked panicked, the strain evident on his face.

"Hi," I said.

"Hi," he choked out.

There were muffled thumps, and we both looked over.

Bissette and Alamanni were on the ground on their stomachs, their wrists tied behind their backs. The bodyguard was tied to a chair.

Vander stood beside him, a handgun in his hand.

"You took your sweet time," Zane said.

"Franz here had hired a few extra guards I didn't know about. Had to take care of them."

"Are they still breathing?" Zane asked.

"Probably. The police are on the way." Vander looked down. "All right there, Monroe?"

"Sure," I said.

"She's been shot in the vest and Franz stabbed her."

Vander finished tying up a sobbing Franz, then knelt beside us. He checked my side and grunted.

"Is that badass speak for I'm bleeding out, or you'll be fine?" I asked.

"You might need a couple of stitches."

I felt nausea climb up my throat. "*No, no, no*. I hate stitches."

"Might?" Zane said. "She got *stabbed*."

"Barely," Vander said. "Looks like the blade caught the edge of the vest. Didn't penetrate too far."

"What?" I squeaked. "I felt it. It hurts."

"She'll be fine."

"Quiet." Zane pulled me closer. "No more talk of being stabbed. I'll relive that moment for the rest of my life."

Warmth bloomed in my chest. "I'm all right, Zane."

He touched his lips to mine. "I'll call my private doctor. We'll see about the stitches."

I felt really queasy now. "I'm sure a bandage will be fine."

He cocked his head.

I waved a hand. "Mag got stitches once. He fell off the monkey bars." I shuddered. "I had to take him to the hospital. The thought of the needle going through my skin—" I shuddered again.

Zane smiled. "You faced down dangerous jewel

thieves and the Russian mafia, but the thought of stitches does you in?"

"Roth—"

He kissed me again. "Don't worry, Wildcat, I'll hold your hand."

Zane

Zane paced his bedroom as his private doctor worked on Monroe.

They were back in his penthouse—it was all shiny, clean, and repaired. The construction crew who'd done the work was one of Liam's and they were good. Zane couldn't tell that his office had been blown up just a few days ago.

He still couldn't get the sight of Monroe's blood spreading on her shirt out of his head.

She'd gotten shot to protect him. The idiot had jumped in front of a bullet for him.

She'd taken a bullet and been stabbed, but had looked more shocked when he'd told her that he was falling for her.

Monroe had lived a lifetime protecting herself, forming that hard, prickly shell of hers.

Well, there was a new protector on the scene.

He was going to take care of her and love her, until she learned not to hunch into a ball, expecting a blow at every turn.

He scraped a hand through his hair. They'd talked

with the police, Vander dealing with most of the questions. They'd watched Franz and the others being taken away in handcuffs.

None of them had mentioned the necklace, which had been safely tucked inside Vander's jacket.

"You're very lucky, young lady," Dr. Thomas said.

The doctor was a middle-aged African-American woman who wore a neat pantsuit. She had short, tight curls, and strong, attractive features.

"The knife didn't penetrate far, and it didn't hit anything vital." The doctor smiled. "You'll only need four stitches."

"What? No." Monroe pushed back against the headboard.

Zane sat on the bed beside her and took her hand. "Come on, Wildcat. It's only four little stitches."

"Four, four thousand." She looked at him, wild-eyed. "It's still a needle going through my skin." She shuddered.

Dr. Thomas pulled some gear out of her medical bag. The color drained from Monroe's face.

"Look at me," he ordered.

Her head swiveled.

"I'll just numb the area," the doctor said.

Monroe shuddered again.

"Vander should be at the meeting with Sidorov now," Zane said.

That got her focus.

"God, I hope Mag's okay." She pressed a hand to her cheek. "I should have gone too—"

Zane's gut cramped at the idea of Monroe anywhere

near the goddamn Russian mafia. "Vander can handle this. In fact, he could handle it with his eyes closed. It's going to be fine."

She blew out a breath. "I really hate waiting."

"He'll be home soon." Zane squeezed her fingers.

She blew out a breath. "That's all thanks to you. I couldn't have done this without you, Zane. You were amazing back there. Where did you learn to fight like that?"

"Liam, Mav, and I do Krav Maga with this crusty, old Israeli trainer. He says he's ex-military, but we think he's a former Mossad spy. He kicks our asses."

She smiled. "So, he's not afraid to kick some prime billionaire butt, huh?"

"Right. That's why I like him. He treats me like a normal person." Zane stroked her jaw. "Just like you have, right from the beginning. You saw *me*, Monroe, not what I have, or could do for you."

She choked out a laugh. "Zane, I came here to—" She looked at the doctor.

"To steal the Phillips-Morley necklace. Don't worry, Dr. Thomas is trustworthy."

"I'm a sphinx." The doctor kept a blank face, leaning over Monroe's side.

"That woman has jabbed me in the butt with a needle too many times for there to be any secrets between us."

Monroe laughed.

"You came here to save your brother, Monroe. I admire that. I love the way you love so strongly."

Dr. Thomas wiped Monroe's side with something and she flinched.

"Look at me," he said.

"I'm looking, but I'm well aware that she has a big needle."

"It's not that big," the doctor drawled.

Monroe whimpered.

Zane knew he needed to pull out the big guns. "I'm falling in love with you, Monroe O'Connor."

Her gray eyes went wide. "No."

"Yes."

"No." She shook her head, looking terrified. It almost made Zane smile.

"You don't get to tell me how I feel." He lowered his mouth to hers and kissed her until she made a sweet little moan. "I love you, Monroe."

Turbulent gray eyes met his—filled with a mix of fear, wonder, and love.

"And you love me back," he added.

She shook her head.

"All done." Dr. Thomas snapped off her gloves.

"What?" Monroe glanced at the doctor, then at the small white bandage on her side. "No way."

"I'm good." The doctor glanced at Zane. "And so is your distraction."

Zane winked.

The doctor moved the sheet, and Zane spotted the massive bruise forming on Monroe's stomach. He cursed.

Dr. Thomas rose. "The bruising's from the bullet she took to the vest. It'll heal, although it'll ache for a while. I'll leave some painkillers for you, Monroe."

"Thank you, Dr. Thomas."

As the doctor disappeared into the bathroom to clean up, Zane shifted closer and pushed the sheet back.

Monroe had gotten this protecting him.

The woman was so in love with him.

He lowered his head and gently kissed the bruise.

"Zane," she murmured.

"I'm not going anywhere, Monroe. I'll be right here, until you're ready to admit that you love me."

There was so much emotion in her eyes. A second later, he heard his phone ding. He pulled it out and saw the message.

"It's from Vander. They're on their way up."

She tensed, pulling in a shaky breath.

"Let's get you dressed," he said.

With Dr. Thomas's help, they got Monroe into one of his loose business shirts, and a pair of her leggings.

They headed out into the living area.

"Take care," the doctor said. "Your pain pills are on the bedside table."

"Thanks again." Monroe's gaze went across to the elevator.

The doors opened and Vander stepped out, followed by a young man, with a mop of black hair.

Maguire O'Connor was probably handsome when he didn't have dark circles under his eyes, and tangled, unwashed hair.

He sheepishly lifted his head, showing off eyes the same gray as his sister's. When he saw Monroe, he froze.

She swallowed. "Mag."

The young man stepped forward. "Monroe—" his voice cracked "—I'm so sorry."

Then Monroe flew across the living room and threw her arms up around her brother. He wrapped his arms around her and hugged her back.

20

PROMISE NOT TO FREAK OUT

Monroe

I held on tight to my brother. Relief rushed through me.

Solid, alive, and breathing.

"I'm so sorry, Mon," Maguire murmured.

"I'm just relieved that you're all right now." I hugged him again, ignoring the twinge in my bruised stomach. "But be warned, Mag, once the relief dulls off a bit, I'm going to be mad. Really mad."

Maguire lifted his head. "My friend, Cy, took me to a card game. I did well at first. You know I like numbers, and cards are easy." He ran a hand down his face. "Then, I didn't do so well. The more I tried to make things right, the deeper in I dug myself."

Anger fizzed in me. "What the *hell* were you thinking?"

"I guess I wasn't thinking. Then I panicked—"

A hand settled on the back of my neck and squeezed.

"You were playing games run by the Russian mafia," Zane said. "They're rigged. They let you win a little to suck you in, then you lose."

Mag looked up, then blinked. "Holy fuck, you're Zane Roth."

Zane nodded. "I'm Monroe's man."

My man? Jeez, if anyone had told me a week or so ago about the hard right turn my life was going to take, I would have peed myself laughing.

Mag blinked, then goggled at me. "You're sleeping with a billionaire?"

"Who I sleep with is no one's business, especially not my baby brother's." I straightened and shot Zane a look. "And he's *not* my...man."

He smiled. "Yes, I am."

"No, you're not. You're stubborn and bossy."

"And you're in love with me." He winked at my brother.

A smile broke out on Mag's face. "Where the hell did you meet a billionaire?"

My mouth dried up. "Well..." I straightened. "It's because of him that you're here." My throat tightened. "He saved you. He helped me, protected me, hired Vander to help, and gave up a priceless necklace to free you."

Mag's smile faded, but my gaze was all for Zane.

"I did it for you, Monroe." Zane cupped my cheeks. "We haven't known each other long, but we've been through a pressure cooker together, and I *know*. You intrigued me from the first moment you tore my towel off and knocked me over."

A laugh escaped me.

"I've learned more about you every minute we've been together. About your business and your work ethic, your loyalty to your friends, the way you love your brother. The way you throw yourself into everything." His thumbs stroked along my cheekbones. "You love so fiercely. I'd give all my wealth for you to love me that way, too."

I felt the burn of tears. "Zane—"

"I'm going to spend every minute proving to you that I'll take care of you. That I'll be there for you when times are good, and when things get tough. I'll try to never let you down."

"Zane, you haven't let me down once. You've stood beside me this last week, through the tough moments. You held me together when I was sure that I'd shatter."

He tugged me against him, and I wrapped my arms around him and breathed him in.

"You're it for me, Monroe O'Connor. I want to grow old with you. I want to hear you laugh, argue with you, love you."

"God." I let my feelings free. "Damn you, Zane Roth, I came to crack your safe and steal a necklace, but you've stolen my heart, instead."

Emotion filled his handsome face. "You stole mine first, Wildcat."

I sucked in a breath. "I love you, Zane. There's no going back now."

"Never. When I make a deal, I keep it." He swept me into his arms, his mouth on mine.

Love was a bright light bursting inside me. I felt the rapid beat of his heart against my chest.

"Mine," he murmured. "Forever."

Forever. I'd never let myself dream of that. I kissed him, then lightly bit his bottom lip.

I looked up and saw Mag touching the corner of his eye. "Are you crying, Mag?"

"What? Hell, no. I'm just happy for my sister."

"Thanks, bro." I leaned into Zane. "Now, you probably need a shower and food."

His eyes lit up. "I'd sell my soul for both." Then his lips flattened, and he shifted on his feet. "I...uh, was staying with Cy. And—"

"No. No more Cy." That young man was trouble. "You can stay at my place."

"You don't have the room—"

"She does," Zane countered, "since Monroe will be here with me."

I frowned. "Here?"

"We just confessed our undying love for each other, Monroe. I want you to move in with me."

My mouth dropped open. Then I closed it. Nope, I couldn't formulate a coherent thought.

Mag laughed. "I've never seen Monroe so lost for words. Ever."

I pointed a finger at him. "Shut it, you."

"Monroe O'Connor living in a fancy, New York City penthouse." Mag shook his head. "Who would have thought it?"

"You're not helping." I glanced at Zane, and saw that he was braced for a fight.

He expected me to argue. To protect myself.

A part of me wanted to do that.

But this man had earned my trust. He'd trusted me when he shouldn't have. He'd done so much to keep me safe and get my brother back.

"I'll move in," I said in a huge rush.

It paid off. That handsome face lit up.

"*Wildcat.*" He scooped me off my feet.

With a laugh, I kissed him.

"You sure you're not going to freak out?" he asked.

"I wouldn't push it, if I were you. I do need to spend some time at Lady Locksmith tomorrow. I've missed work, and Sabrina's been picking up the slack." I looked at my brother. "You're going to clean the stock room, and sweep the shop until it's sparkling. You can work at Lady Locksmith until you find a job."

He nodded.

"What work are you good at?" Zane asked.

Mag shrugged. "Um, I'm not sure. I'm good with numbers, and I like math."

Zane smiled. "Me, too. Let's talk."

Monroe

I finished putting some small home safes on the shelf. *There.*

Setting my hands on my hips, I smiled.

The shop looked great. Two people were browsing, and my locksmiths were all out on jobs. Business was ticking along nicely. The thought of expanding crossed my mind, and I grinned. I'd love to open another shop, and hire some more locksmiths.

One day.

Whistling echoed from the back room and my smile widened. Mag was cleaning the stock room. I'd gotten him settled in my apartment, and he had a meeting set to talk with Zane about some potential jobs at Roth Enterprises.

Zane had made me pack a suitcase of things. We planned to move the rest of my stuff to his place on the weekend.

I paused. Strangely, that thought only caused a minor heart palpitation. Mainly, it made me want to smile.

I was in love with a hot guy who loved me back. Life was good.

The door chimed.

Sabrina sailed in. Her blue eyes zeroed in on me like heat-seeking missiles. "You've been avoiding me."

"I haven't. I've been busy. Mag...really screwed up."

Concern instantly filled Sabrina's face. "Is he okay?"

"He is now. He's out back, cleaning the stock room."

"Good." My best friend lifted her chin. "And do you have a date for my wedding?"

I hadn't actually asked Zane to go to the wedding with me yet, but I knew he'd say yes. I opened my mouth—

Sabrina lifted her hands. "No excuses, Monroe. No more dodging, ducking, or weaving."

"Sab—"

"Nope. I warned you that if you didn't find someone,

I would. Andrew has a nice cousin. He still lives at home, but he has a good job. He's a payroll manager—"

"I have a date."

Falling silent, Sabrina stared, her gaze narrowing. "Who?"

"Well, he's a really great guy—"

"What's he do?"

"Um, he's...in finance?"

Her gaze narrowed more. "You're being cagey."

"Sabrina, you have to promise not to freak out."

My friend cocked a hip. "I don't freak out."

I raised my brows.

Sabrina pulled a face. "Okay, okay, sometimes I freak out. *Wait*. It isn't one of Maguire's friends, is it?" Vague horror filled her eyes.

"No, but Mag's indirectly responsible for us meeting."

"Okay, so who are you bringing to my wedding?"

I took a deep breath. "Zane Roth."

Sabrina stared at me for a blink, then burst out laughing.

I rolled my eyes.

She bent over, still laughing. "Good one. Okay, tell me for real, now."

"I'm not joking."

My best friend's nose wrinkled "You still don't have a date, and you're trying to distract me. *Monroe*."

"Sabrina, I—"

The door chimed, and the man in question strode in. He was taking me to lunch.

As always, he looked hot, and all my girl parts took

notice. The man was walking suit porn in a tailored, black suit, pale shirt, and tie.

He saw me and smiled.

I smiled back.

"Hey, Wildcat." He walked toward me, slid an arm around my waist, and touched his lips to mine.

I heard a sound—sort of a cross between a gurgle and a choking noise.

Sabrina stared at Zane.

She blinked and made another alien noise.

"Hey." I waved my hand at her. "Sabrina, this is Zane. Zane, this is my usually normal friend, Sabrina."

"It's a pleasure to meet you, Sabrina," he said.

Sabrina held up a hand. "I need a minute."

We waited.

She opened her mouth, then shook her head. "Nope. Not yet."

Mag popped his head out of the back room. "Hey, Zane."

"Hi, Mag."

Sabrina made another sound.

With an amused half grin, Zane glanced down at me. "Are you ready for lunch?"

"I'm starving."

"Why don't we take another load of your things to my place, too?"

"Sure."

"Wait," Sabrina said. "Your things to his place?"

"Um." I tucked a strand of hair back behind my ear. "I'm moving in with Zane."

Sabrina sagged against the counter. "I need more than a minute. Maybe an hour, or a week."

Zane slid an arm across my shoulders. "Take as long as you need. I'm not going anywhere."

Looking at us, Sabrina's face warmed. "All right, Monroe O'Connor, you need to tell me *exactly* how you met and snagged a billionaire bachelor."

"I'm not a bachelor anymore," Zane said. "And I think I snagged her."

"It's a long story." I smiled at my man. I knew we'd grow old together, love, laugh, and cry together, but most importantly, we'd always be there for each other. No matter what.

"Then you better start talking," Sabrina demanded.

With a laugh, Zane kissed me again.

Zane

Zane sipped his Scotch, the ice tinkling in the glass.

Mayfair looked as classy as ever, but tonight, the club's dance floor was not wall-to-wall with people.

The music was on low for the exclusive cocktail party for Nightingale House.

It had been Monroe's idea. He smiled. His woman had expertly badgered Liam to use his club for the event.

Looking around, Zane noted that it was mostly women, with a few men. Some looked nervous, and uncertain, but they were slowly relaxing. Nearby, he saw one woman sipping a cocktail cautiously, while another tugged at the hem of her little black dress.

Monroe had wanted to raise money for the shelter, but also give the survivors a night out to relax, have fun, and feel normal.

It hadn't taken much for her to convince Liam. Kensington had swung into gear and organized everything for the party. He'd roped in some of his marketing team from Kensington Group. The team had planned everything with military precision, including approaching the right people for donations.

Monroe had arranged an experienced team of babysitters to care for the kids at the shelter so their moms, and a few dads, could attend. Sabrina had also gotten involved to provide party clothes for everyone to borrow.

Zane had donated a substantial amount to Nightingale House. When Monroe had found out the other morning—after a shocked and grateful Nightingale House director had called her—Monroe had been flabbergasted and a little annoyed that he hadn't told her.

"I'm not doing anything for this party." He kissed her nose. "I wanted to help, and this was the easiest way I could."

She'd scrunched up her nose, but kissed him.

He searched the club for her and found her easily—it was like he had an in-built radar for all things Monroe O'Connor.

She was talking animatedly with some women, Sabrina and her fiancé, and Simeon.

Zane's trainer was dressed up in a dark suit, with his

wife beside him. Simeon had offered to run some self-defense courses at Nightingale House.

Zane's mom was there as well. She was listening as Monroe spoke, nodding and smiling.

His gaze locked on Monroe. She was wearing that sexy red dress that she'd worn before. It hugged her curves and left those slim shoulders bare. He'd always been an ass and legs man before, but suddenly he was a shoulders man as well.

She turned and smiled at him.

He felt it deep in his gut.

Behind her, Simeon winked at Zane. His mom smiled, a satisfied look on her face. She was wearing her new necklace. It was a replica of the Phillips-Morley that he'd had designed just for her.

Monroe broke away from the group and sauntered toward him.

"Thank you," she murmured.

"For what?"

She pressed her hands to his chest. "Loving me."

Zane kissed her. "You make it easy."

"God, you can't keep your hands off the woman." Mav appeared, and despite his grumbling, his lips were tipped into a smile.

Monroe poked her tongue at him.

Several days this week, Monroe had been busy consulting at Rivera Tech. Mav had thawed toward Zane's woman, no longer convinced that Monroe was after his money. And as they'd talked security and safes, the pair had bonded.

"Yes," Zane said. "I can't keep my hands off her, and I can't wait to get her home tonight and—"

Monroe snatched a canapé off a table nearby and shoved it in his mouth.

"Be happy there's no sea urchin in that," she said.

"Hey." Rollo appeared. "Have you tried these fried things?" He was holding a plate loaded with canapés. "Man, they are *so* good." He popped two in his mouth.

The geek hacker was wearing a burgundy, velvet suit and had on a bright yellow bowtie. He hadn't bothered to brush his wild hair, and tonight he wore glasses that made his eyes look huge.

"You need a drink, Rollo?" Mav asked.

Rollo was also working at Rivera Tech and enjoying the hell out of himself.

"They have Red Bull?"

"Sure," Mav said.

"Let's go, my man."

As they headed for the bar, Maguire and Liam emerged from the crowd.

"Everything running smoothly?" Liam asked.

"Thanks to you." Monroe went up on her toes and kissed Liam's cheek. "Thank you for everything you've done. Your marketing team are brilliant."

The Kensington Group team was nearby—several women and two men. They were decked out in designer dresses and were sharing cocktails.

"I only hire the best," Liam said.

"And they're hot," Mag said quietly, eyeing the women.

Monroe's brother was doing well after his misadventure. He'd started an internship at Roth Enterprises. He had a probationary period, and knew he had to do well and prove himself to earn a full-time position in Zane's company.

Zane had spent time with him. Maguire was bright, good with numbers, and hungry for guidance.

"It's my pleasure, Monroe." Liam ran his hand down her arm. "You've done an amazing job organizing this event."

"Hey, quit flirting with my girl," Zane grumbled. "Get your own."

Liam smiled, as charming as ever. "But there's so much variety to enjoy."

Zane snorted, but knew that Liam had his own scars, and felt much like Zane had before Monroe. Nothing and no one captured his interest.

Monroe rolled her eyes. "Well, the one thing I've learned is that love hits you when you least expect it, and often in the middle of the worst circumstances." Her gaze met Zane's. "And it's the best thing that can ever happen to you."

He cupped her face, chest filled with warmth.

Mag pulled a face. "Jeez, my tough, safe-cracking sister has gone all Hallmark."

Monroe punched her brother in the arm and made him laugh.

"Get away from me, Johnny!"

A woman's terrified voice broke through the party.

They all spun.

Across the room, a tall man gripped a middle-aged woman by the front of her dress, tugging her up on her toes. "You're mine, Leigh. You're not fucking leaving me!"

What the hell? Zane tensed. The man was wearing a bartender uniform. Ah hell, some asshole had snuck in to get to one of the Nightingale House women.

The man shoved the woman, and she slammed into a table. Glasses fell and smashed. Screams broke out.

"Security," Liam yelled.

"Stay back." Zane shoved Monroe toward Maguire.

Zane and Liam started forward. He saw Mav closing in from the other side.

Johnny raised his big fists, and the woman cowered.

Fuck. They were too far away to stop him.

Suddenly, a blonde woman in a short, tight green dress appeared beside the enraged man. She kicked the guy right between the legs.

The man yelped and bent over.

The blonde woman pivoted, then pressed a hand to the back of the guy's head. With a quick push, she slammed his face into the table.

The man let out a strangled shout, blood pouring from his nose.

The woman followed with a hard punch to the man's gut.

He dropped to his knees.

"You shouldn't pick on defenseless people," the woman in green bit out.

Simeon reached them first. He drove the man face down to the floor, then glanced up at the woman. "Nice moves."

Fucking amazing moves. Zane stopped beside the woman. "Good job."

She stepped back. "I've taken some self-defense classes. Every woman in New York should."

Liam, a frown on his face, stepped toward her. "Are you okay?"

"I'm fine, Mr. Kensington. Nothing a vodka martini won't help." She smiled. The woman had strong features, with bright green eyes, and a sexy cleft in the center of her chin. Her hair was almost platinum blonde, falling past her shoulders. She wasn't pretty or beautiful exactly, but definitely attractive.

When one of the Kensington Group team raced over, Zane realized the woman was one of Liam's marketing employees.

"Oh my God." A woman in a gold dress gripped the blonde's arm. "Are you okay?"

"Totally fine."

"I don't know your name," Liam said.

"I'm Penn. I'm new. I just started last week."

The man's ex-wife, Leigh, was sobbing quietly, being consoled by some of the other women.

"I hope she's okay." Penn turned and strode back to the other Kensington Group employees. Liam stared after her.

"Liam?" Zane said. "Liam? Earth to Kensington."

"What?" Liam swiveled, still frowning. He shook his head, then waved at the security guards. The security team dragged a bleeding Johnny out.

Then Liam turned to Leigh, who was dabbing her tears away.

"I'm very sorry for that. He should never have gotten in here."

"Oh, no, it's my fault. I —"

"No. It's not." Liam offered her his arm. "How about a drink?"

The older woman gave him a watery smile. "I've never had a drink with a billionaire."

Liam flashed her his most charming smile. "Today's the day."

He led the now-smiling woman to the bar, but Zane noted that his friend was glancing over at the Kensington Group table. Or more specifically, at one blonde in green.

"Well, that could've turned bad." Monroe pressed into Zane's side.

He pulled her close. "Everyone's fine."

Around them, the party was resuming. Conversations restarted, and some people were venturing onto the dance floor.

"Let's hope there's no more drama." He nipped her lips. "Because I really want to take my wildcat home. That dress..." He made a sound.

She rubbed against him. "Remember the last time I wore this dress?"

"We are not having phone sex tonight, O'Connor. No, tonight you're all mine."

"I'm always yours."

She was. And he knew she'd be his forever. "I love you, Monroe."

"I love you, too. Stealing from a billionaire was the best thing I ever did."

Laughing, Zane closed his mouth over hers.

I hope you enjoyed Monroe and Zane's story!

The **Billionaire Heists Trilogy** continues with *Blackmailing Mr. Bossman*, starring billionaire Liam Kensington and a certain blonde in green, releasing next month, on the 22nd June 2021.

Want to know more about Vander Norcross? Then check out the first book in the Norcross Security series, *The Investigator*, starring Vander's brother Rhys. **Read on for a preview of the first chapter.**

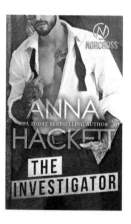

Don't miss out! For updates about new releases, free books, and other fun stuff, sign up for my VIP mailing list and get your *free box set* containing three action-packed romances.

Visit here to get started: www.annahackett.com

Would you like
a FREE BOX SET
of my books?

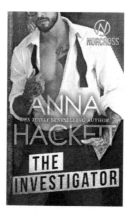

There was a glass of chardonnay with her name on it waiting for her at home.

Haven McKinney smiled. The museum was closed, and she was *done* for the day.

As she walked across the East gallery of the Hutton Museum, her heels clicked on the marble floor.

God, she loved the place. The creamy marble that made up the flooring and wrapped around the grand pillars was gorgeous. It had that hushed air of grandeur that made her heart squeeze a little every time she stepped inside. But more than that, the amazing art the Hutton housed sang to the art lover in her blood.

Snagging a job here as the curator six months ago had been a dream come true. She'd been at a low point in her life. Very low. Haven swallowed a snort and circled a stunning white-marble sculpture of a naked, reclining woman with the most perfect resting bitch face. She'd never guessed that her life would come crashing down at age twenty-nine.

She lifted her chin. Miami was her past. The Hutton and San Francisco were her future. No more throwing caution to the wind. She had a plan, and she was sticking to it.

She paused in front of a stunning exhibit of traditional Chinese painting and calligraphy. It was one of their newer exhibits, and had been Haven's brainchild. Nearby, an interactive display was partially assembled. Over the next few days, her staff would finish the installation. Excitement zipped through Haven. She couldn't wait to have the touchscreens operational. It was her passion to make art more accessible, especially to children. To help them be a part of it, not just look at it. To learn, to feel, to enjoy.

Art had helped her through some of the toughest times in her life, and she wanted to share that with others.

She looked at the gorgeous old paintings again. One portrayed a mountainous landscape with beautiful maple trees. It soothed her nerves.

Wine would soothe her nerves, as well. *Right.* She

needed to get upstairs to her office and grab her handbag, then get an Uber home.

Her cell phone rang and she unclipped it from the lanyard she wore at the museum. "Hello?"

"Change of plans, girlfriend," a smoky female voice said. "Let's go out and celebrate being gorgeous, successful, and single. I'm done at the office, and believe me, it has been a *grueling* day."

Haven smiled at her new best friend. She'd met Gia Norcross when she joined the Hutton. Gia's wealthy brother, Easton Norcross, owned the museum, and was Haven's boss. The museum was just a small asset in the businessman's empire. Haven suspected Easton owned at least a third of San Francisco. Maybe half.

She liked and respected her boss. Easton could be tough, but he valued her opinions. And she loved his bossy, take-charge, energetic sister. Gia ran a highly successful PR firm in the city, and did all the PR and advertising for the Hutton. They'd met not long after Haven had started work at the museum.

After their first meeting, Gia had dragged Haven out to her favorite restaurant and bar, and the rest was history.

"I guess making people's Instagram look pretty and not staged is hard work," Haven said with a grin.

"Bitch." Gia laughed. "God, I had a meeting with a businessman caught in...well, let's just say he and his assistant were *not* taking notes on the boardroom table."

Haven felt an old, unwelcome memory rise up. She mentally stomped it down. "I don't feel sorry for the cheating asshole, I feel sorry for whatever poor shmuck got more than they were paid for when they walked into the boardroom."

"Actually, it was the cheating businessman's wife."

"Uh-oh."

"And the assistant was male," Gia added.

"Double uh-oh."

"Then said cheater comes to my PR firm, telling me to clean up his mess, because he's thinking he might run for governor one day. I mean, I'm good, but I can't wrangle miracles."

Haven suspected that Gia had verbally eviscerated the man and sent him on his way. Gia Norcross had a sharp tongue, and wasn't afraid to use it.

"So, grueling day and I need alcohol. I'll meet you at ONE65, and the first drink is on me."

"I'm pretty wiped, Gia—"

"Uh-uh, no excuses. I'll see you in an hour." And with that, Gia was gone.

Haven clipped her phone to her lanyard. Well, it looked like she was having that chardonnay at ONE65, the six-story, French dining experience Gia loved. Each level offered something different, from patisserie, to bistro and grill, to bar and lounge.

Haven walked into the museum's main gallery, and her blood pressure dropped to a more normal level. It was her favorite space in the museum. The smell of wood, the gorgeous lights gleaming overhead, and the amazing paintings combined to create a soothing room. She smoothed her hands down her fitted, black skirt. Haven was tall, at five foot eight, and curvy, just like her mom had been. Her boobs, currently covered by a cute, white blouse with a tie around her neck, weren't much to write home about, but she had to buy her skirts one size bigger. She sighed. No matter how much she walked or jogged —*blergh*, okay, she didn't jog much—she still had an ass.

Even in her last couple of months in Miami, when stress had caused her to lose a bunch of weight due to everything going on, her ass hadn't budged.

Memories of Miami—and her douchebag-of-epic-proportions-ex—threatened, churning like storm clouds on the horizon.

Nope. She locked those thoughts down. She was *not* going there.

She had a plan, and the number one thing for taking back and rebuilding her life was *no* men. She'd sworn off anyone with a Y chromosome.

She didn't need one, didn't want one, she was D-O-N-E, done.

She stopped in front of the museum's star attraction. Claude Monet's *Water Lilies*.

Haven loved the impressionist's work. She loved the colors, the delicate strokes. This one depicted water lilies and lily pads floating on a gentle pond. His paintings always made an impact, and had a haunting, yet soothing feel to them.

It was also worth just over a hundred million dollars.

The price tag still made her heart flutter. She'd put a business case to Easton, and they'd purchased the painting three weeks ago at auction. Haven had planned out the display down to the rivets used on the wood. She'd thrown herself into the project.

Gia had put together a killer marketing campaign,

and Haven had reluctantly been interviewed by the local paper. But it had paid off. Ticket sales to the museum were up, and everyone wanted to see *Water Lilies*.

Footsteps echoed through the empty museum, and she turned to see a uniformed security guard appear in the doorway.

"Ms. McKinney?"

"Yes, David? I was just getting ready to leave."

"Sorry to delay you. There's a delivery truck at the back entrance. They say they have a delivery of a Zadkine bronze."

Haven frowned, running through the next day's schedule in her head. "That's due tomorrow."

"It sounds like they had some other deliveries nearby and thought they'd squeeze it in."

She glanced at her slim, silver wristwatch, fighting back annoyance. She'd had a long day, and now she'd be late to meet Gia. "Fine. Have them bring it in."

With a nod, David disappeared. Haven pulled out her phone and quickly fired off a text to warn Gia that she'd be late. Then Haven headed up to her office, and checked her notes for tomorrow. She had several calls to make to chase down some pieces for a new exhibit she wanted to launch in the winter. There were some restoration quotes to go over, and a charity gala for her art charity to plan. She needed to get down into the storage rooms and see if there was anything they could cycle out and put on display.

God, she loved her job. Not many people would get excited about digging around in dusty storage rooms, but Haven couldn't wait.

She made sure her laptop was off and grabbed her handbag. She slipped her lanyard off and stuffed her phone in her bag.

When she reached the bottom of the stairs, she heard a strange noise from the gallery. A muffled pop, then a thump.

Frowning, she took one step toward the gallery.

Suddenly, David staggered through the doorway, a splotch of red on his shirt.

Haven's pulse spiked. *Oh God, was that blood?* "David—"

"Run." He collapsed to the floor.

Fear choking her, she kicked off her heels and spun. She had to get help.

But she'd only taken two steps when a hand sank into her hair, pulling her neat twist loose, and sending her brown hair cascading over her shoulders.

"Let me go!"

She was dragged into the main gallery, and when she lifted her head, her gut churned.

Five men dressed in black, all wearing balaclavas, stood in a small group.

No...oh, no.

Their other guard, Gus, stood with his hands in the air. He was older, former military. She was shoved closer toward him.

"Ms. McKinney, you okay?" Gus asked.

She managed a nod. "They shot David."

"I kn—"

"No talking," one man growled.

Haven lifted her chin. "What do you want?" There was a slight quaver in her voice.

The man who'd grabbed her glared. His cold, blue eyes glittered through the slits in his balaclava. Then he ignored her, and with the others, they turned to face the *Water Lilies*.

Haven's stomach dropped. *No.* This couldn't be happening.

A thin man moved forward, studying the painting's gilt frame with gloved hands. "It's wired to an alarm."

Blue Eyes, clearly the group's leader, turned and aimed the gun at Gus' barrel chest. "Disconnect it."

"No," the guard said belligerently.

"I'm not asking."

Haven held up her hands. "Please—"

The gun fired. Gus dropped to one knee, pressing a hand to his shoulder.

"No!" she cried.

The leader stepped forward and pressed the gun to the older man's head.

"No." Haven fought back her fear and panic. "Don't hurt him. I'll disconnect it."

Slowly, she inched toward the painting, carefully avoiding the thin man still standing close to it. She touched the security panel built in beside the frame, pressing her palm to the small pad.

A second later, there was a discreet beep.

Two other men came forward and grabbed the frame.

She glanced around at them. "You're making a mistake. If you know who owns this museum, then you know you won't get away with this." Who would go up against the Norcross family? Easton, rich as sin, had a lot of connections, but his brother, Vander... Haven suppressed a shiver. Gia's middle brother might be hot, but he scared the bejesus out of Haven.

Vander Norcross, former military badass, owned Norcross Security and Investigations. His team had put in the high-tech security for the museum.

No one in their right mind wanted to go up against Vander, or the third Norcross brother who also worked with Vander, or the rest of Vander's team of badasses.

"Look, if you just—"

The blow to her head made her stagger. She blinked, pain radiating through her face. Blue Eyes had back-handed her.

He moved in and hit her again, and Haven cried out, clutching her face. It wasn't the first time she'd been hit. Her douchebag ex had hit her once. That was the day she'd left him for good.

But this was worse. Way worse.

"Shut up, you stupid bitch."

The next blow sent her to the floor. She thought she heard someone chuckle. He followed with a kick to her ribs, and Haven curled into a ball, a sob in her throat.

Her vision wavered and she blinked. Blue Eyes crouched down, putting his hand to the tiles right in front of her. Dizziness hit her, and she vaguely took in the freckles on the man's hand. They formed a spiral pattern.

"No one talks back to me," the man growled. "Especially a woman." He moved away.

She saw the men were busy maneuvering the painting off the wall. It was easy for two people to move.

She knew its exact dimensions—eighty by one hundred centimeters.

No one was paying any attention to her. Fighting through the nausea and dizziness, she dragged herself a few inches across the floor, closer to the nearby pillar. A pillar that had one of several hidden, high-tech panic buttons built into it.

When the men were turned away, she reached up and pressed the button.

Then blackness sucked her under.

HAVEN SAT on one of the lovely wooden benches she'd had installed around the museum. She'd wanted somewhere for guests to sit and take in the art.

She'd never expected to be sitting on one, holding a melting ice pack to her throbbing face, and staring at the empty wall where a multi-million-dollar masterpiece should be hanging. And she definitely didn't expect to be doing it with police dusting black powder all over the museum's walls.

Tears pricked her eyes. She was alive, her guards were hurt but alive, and that was what mattered. The police had questioned her and she'd told them everything she could remember. The paramedics had checked her over and given her the ice pack. Nothing was broken, but she'd been told to expect swelling and bruising.

David and Gus had been taken to the hospital. She'd been assured the men would be okay. Last she'd heard, David was in surgery. Her throat tightened. *Oh, God.*

What was she going to tell Easton?

Haven bit her lip and a tear fell down her cheek. She hadn't cried in months. She'd shed more than enough tears over Leo after he'd gone crazy and hit her. She'd left Miami the next day. She'd needed to get away from her ex and, unfortunately, despite loving her job at a classy Miami art gallery, Leo's cousin had owned it. Alyssa had been the one who had introduced them.

Haven had learned a painful lesson to not mix business and pleasure.

She'd been done with Leo's growing moodiness, outbursts, and cheating on her and hitting her had been the last straw. *Asshole.*

She wiped the tear away. San Francisco was as far from Miami as she could get and still be in the continental US. This was supposed to be her fresh new start.

She heard footsteps—solid, quick, and purposeful. Easton strode in.

He was a tall man, with dark hair that curled at the collar of his perfectly fitted suit. Haven had sworn off men, but she was still woman enough to appreciate her boss' good looks. His mother was Italian-American, and she'd passed down her very good genes to her children.

Like his brothers, Easton had been in the military, too, although he'd joined the Army Rangers. It showed in his muscled body. Once, she'd seen his shirt sleeves rolled up when they'd had a late meeting. He had some interesting ink that was totally at odds with his sophisticated-businessman persona.

His gaze swept the room, his jaw tight. It settled on her and he strode over.

"Haven—"

"Oh God, Easton. I'm so sorry."

He sat beside her and took her free hand. He squeezed her cold fingers, then he looked at her face and cursed.

She hadn't been brave enough to look in the mirror, but she guessed it was bad.

"They took the *Water Lilies*," she said.

"Okay, don't worry about it just now."

She gave a hiccupping laugh. "Don't worry? It's worth a hundred and ten *million* dollars."

A muscle ticked in his jaw. "You're okay, and that's the main thing. And the guards are in serious but stable condition at the hospital."

She nodded numbly. "It's all my fault."

Easton's gaze went to the police, and then moved back to her. "That's not true."

"I let them in." Her voice broke. God, she wanted the marble floor to crack and swallow her.

"Don't worry." Easton's face turned very serious. "Vander and Rhys will find the painting."

Her boss' tone made her shiver. Something made her suspect that Easton wanted his brothers to find the men who'd stolen the painting more than recovering the priceless piece of art.

She licked her lips, and felt the skin on her cheek tug. She'd have some spectacular bruises later. *Great. Thanks, universe.*

Then Easton's head jerked up, and Haven followed his gaze.

A man stood in the doorway. She hadn't heard him

coming. Nope, Vander Norcross moved silently, like a ghost.

He was a few inches over six feet, had a powerful body, and radiated authority. His suit didn't do much to tone down the sense that a predator had stalked into the room. While Easton was handsome, Vander wasn't. His face was too rugged, and while both he and Easton had blue eyes, Vander's were dark indigo, and as cold as the deepest ocean depths.

He didn't look happy. She fought back a shiver.

Then another man stepped up beside Vander.

Haven's chest locked. *Oh, no. No, no, no.*

She should have known. He was Vander's top investigator. Rhys Matteo Norcross, the youngest of the Norcross brothers.

At first glance, he looked like his brothers—similar build, muscular body, dark hair and bronze skin. But Rhys was the youngest, and he had a charming edge his brothers didn't share. He smiled more frequently, and his shaggy, thick hair always made her imagine him as a rock star, holding a guitar and making girls scream.

Haven was also totally, one hundred percent in lust with him. Any time he got near, he made her body flare to life, her heart beat faster, and made her brain freeze up. She could barely talk around the man.

She did *not* want Rhys Norcross to notice her. Or talk to her. Or turn his soulful, brown eyes her way.

Nuh-uh. No way. She'd sworn off men. This one should have a giant warning sign hanging on him. *Watch out, heartbreak waiting to happen.*

Rhys had been in the military with Vander. Some

hush-hush special unit that no one talked about. Now he worked at Norcross Security—apparently finding anything and anyone.

He also raced cars and boats in his free time. The man liked to go fast. Oh, and he bedded women. His reputation was legendary. Rhys liked a variety of adventures and experiences.

It was lucky Haven had sworn off men.

Especially when they happened to be her boss' brother.

And especially, especially when they were also her best friend's brother.

Off limits.

She saw the pair turn to look her and Easton's way.

Crap. Pulse racing, she looked at her bare feet and red toenails, which made her realize she hadn't recovered her shoes yet. They were her favorites.

She felt the men looking at her, and like she was drawn by a magnet, she looked up. Vander was scowling. Rhys' dark gaze was locked on her.

Haven's traitorous heart did a little tango in her chest.

Before she knew what was happening, Rhys went down on one knee in front of her.

She saw rage twist his handsome features. Then he shocked her by cupping her jaw, and pushing the ice pack away.

They'd never talked much. At Gia's parties, Haven purposely avoided him. He'd never touched her before, and she felt the warmth of him singe through her.

His eyes flashed. "It's going to be okay, baby."

Baby?

He stroked her cheekbone, those long fingers gentle.

Fighting for some control, Haven closed her hand over his wrist. She swallowed. "I—"

"Don't worry, Haven. I'm going to find the man who did this to you and make him regret it."

Her belly tightened. *Oh, God.* When was the last time anyone had looked out for her like this? She was certain no one had ever promised to hunt anyone down for her. Her gaze dropped to his lips.

He had amazingly shaped lips, a little fuller than such a tough man should have, framed by dark stubble.

There was a shift in his eyes and his face warmed. His fingers kept stroking her skin and she felt that caress all over.

Then she heard the click of heels moving at speed. Gia burst into the room.

"What the hell is going on?"

Haven jerked back from Rhys and his hypnotic touch. Damn, she'd been proven right—she was so weak where this man was concerned.

Gia hurried toward them. She was five-foot-four, with a curvy, little body, and a mass of dark, curly hair. As usual, she wore one of her power suits—short skirt, fitted jacket, and sky-high heels.

"Out of my way." Gia shouldered Rhys aside. When her friend got a look at Haven, her mouth twisted. "I'm going to *kill* them."

"Gia," Vander said. "The place is filled with cops. Maybe keep your plans for murder and vengeance quiet."

"Fix this." She pointed at Vander's chest, then at

Rhys. Then she turned and hugged Haven. "You're coming home with me."

"Gia—"

"No. No arguments." Gia held up her palm like a traffic cop. Haven had seen "the hand" before. It was pointless arguing.

Besides, she realized she didn't want to be alone. And the quicker she got away from Rhys' dark, far-too-perceptive gaze, the better.

Norcross Security

The Investigator
The Troubleshooter
The Specialist
The Bodyguard

PREVIEW: TEAM 52 AND THS

W ant to learn more about the mysterious, covert *Team 52?* Check out the first book in the series, *Mission: Her Protection.*

When Rowan's Arctic research team pulls a strange object out of the ice in Northern

Canada, things start to go wrong…very, very wrong. Rescued by a covert, black ops team, she finds herself in the powerful arms of a man with scary gold eyes. A man who vows to do everything and anything to protect her…

Dr. Rowan Schafer has learned it's best to do things herself and not depend on anyone else. Her cold, academic parents taught her that lesson. She loves the challenge of running a research base, until the day her scientists discover the object in a retreating glacier. Under attack, Rowan finds herself fighting to survive… until the mysterious Team 52 arrives.

Former special forces Marine Lachlan Hunter's military career ended in blood and screams, until he was recruited to lead a special team. A team tasked with a top-secret mission—to secure and safeguard pieces of powerful ancient technology. Married to his job, he's done too much and seen too much to risk inflicting his demons on a woman. But when his team arrives in the Arctic, he uncovers both an unexplained artifact, and a young girl from his past, now all grown up. A woman who ignites emotions inside him like never before.

But as Team 52 heads back to their base in Nevada, other hostile forces are after the artifact. Rowan finds herself under attack, and as the bullets fly, Lachlan vows to protect her at all costs. But in the face of danger like they've never seen before, will it be enough to keep her alive.

Team 52

Mission: Her Protection
Mission: Her Rescue
Mission: Her Security
Mission: Her Defense
Mission: Her Safety
Mission: Her Freedom
Mission: Her Shield
Also Available as Audiobooks!

Want to learn more about *Treasure Hunter Security?* Check out the first book in the series, *Undiscovered,* Declan Ward's action-packed story.

One former Navy SEAL. One dedicated archeologist. One secret map to a fabulous lost oasis.

Finding undiscovered treasures is always daring, dangerous, and deadly. Perfect for the men of Treasure Hunter Security. Former Navy SEAL Declan Ward is haunted by the demons of his past and throws everything he has into his security business—Treasure Hunter Security. Dangerous archeological digs – no problem. Daring expeditions – sure thing. Museum security for invaluable exhibits – easy. But on a simple dig in the Egyptian desert, he collides with a stubborn, smart archeologist, Dr. Layne Rush, and together they get swept into a deadly treasure hunt for a mythical lost oasis. When an evil from his past reappears, Declan vows to do anything to protect Layne.

Dr. Layne Rush is dedicated to building a successful career—a promise to the parents she lost far too young. But when her dig is plagued by strange accidents, targeted by a lethal black market antiquities ring, and artifacts are stolen, she is forced to turn to Treasure Hunter Security, and to the tough, sexy, and too-used-to-giving-orders Declan. Soon her organized dig morphs into a wild treasure hunt across the desert dunes.

Danger is hunting them every step of the way, and Layne and Declan must find a way to work together...to not only find the treasure but to survive.

Treasure Hunter Security
Undiscovered
Uncharted
Unexplored
Unfathomed

Untraveled
Unmapped
Unidentified
Undetected
Also Available as Audiobooks!

ALSO BY ANNA HACKETT

Norcross Security

The Investigator

The Troubleshooter

The Specialist

The Bodyguard

Team 52

Mission: Her Protection

Mission: Her Rescue

Mission: Her Security

Mission: Her Defense

Mission: Her Safety

Mission: Her Freedom

Mission: Her Shield

Mission: Her Justice

Also Available as Audiobooks!

Treasure Hunter Security

Undiscovered

Uncharted

Unexplored

Unfathomed

Untraveled

Unmapped

Unidentified

Undetected

Also Available as Audiobooks!

Eon Warriors

Edge of Eon

Touch of Eon

Heart of Eon

Kiss of Eon

Mark of Eon

Claim of Eon

Storm of Eon

Soul of Eon

Also Available as Audiobooks!

Galactic Gladiators: House of Rone

Sentinel

Defender

Centurion

Paladin

Guard

Weapons Master

Also Available as Audiobooks!

Galactic Gladiators

Gladiator

Warrior

Hero

Protector

Champion

Barbarian

Beast

Rogue

Guardian

Cyborg

Imperator

Hunter

Also Available as Audiobooks!

Hell Squad

Marcus

Cruz

Gabe

Reed

Roth

Noah

Shaw

Holmes

Niko

Finn

Theron

Hemi

Ash

Levi

Manu

Griff

Dom

Survivors

Tane

Also Available as Audiobooks!

The Anomaly Series

Time Thief

Mind Raider

Soul Stealer

Salvation

Anomaly Series Box Set

The Phoenix Adventures

Among Galactic Ruins

At Star's End

In the Devil's Nebula

On a Rogue Planet

Beneath a Trojan Moon

Beyond Galaxy's Edge

On a Cyborg Planet

Return to Dark Earth

On a Barbarian World

Lost in Barbarian Space

Through Uncharted Space

Crashed on an Ice World

Perma Series

Winter Fusion

A Galactic Holiday

Warriors of the Wind

Tempest

Storm & Seduction

Fury & Darkness

Standalone Titles

Savage Dragon

Hunter's Surrender

One Night with the Wolf

For more information visit www.annahackett.com

ABOUT THE AUTHOR

I'm a USA Today bestselling romance author who's passionate about *fast-paced, emotion-filled* contemporary and science fiction romance. I love writing about people overcoming unbeatable odds and achieving seemingly impossible goals. I like to believe it's possible for all of us to do the same.

I live in Australia with my own personal hero and two very busy, always-on-the-move sons.

For release dates, behind-the-scenes info, free books, and other fun stuff, sign up for the latest news here:

Website: www.annahackett.com

Printed in Great Britain
by Amazon